James Rice, Sir Besant

The Case of Mr. Lucraft, and Other Tales

Vol. 1

James Rice, Sir Besant

The Case of Mr. Lucraft, and Other Tales
Vol. 1

ISBN/EAN: 9783337088828

Printed in Europe, USA, Canada, Australia, Japan

Cover: Foto ©Andreas Hilbeck / pixelio.de

More available books at **www.hansebooks.com**

MR. L

OTHER T

THE AUTHOR
DBOY," "
BUTTER

IN TWO VOLUMES.

VOL. I.

LONDON:

SAMPSON LOW, MARSTON, SEARLE & RIVINGTON,

CROWN BUILDINGS, 188, FLEET STREET.

1876.

CONTENTS OF VOLUME I.

———◆◆———

PART I.

FROM THE SUPERNATURAL.

PREFACE.

WHEN Jules Janin once published a collection
of tales which, as he modestly owned, would
leave nothing behind them when once read,
he asked himself why he was putting them
together for publication. And the best
answer he could find was, "C'est son Altesse
ma Vanité qui le veut ainsi." He goes on
to say that the reader may be very well content with this motive, "qui est le grand fond
de tous les caractères et de toutes les œuvres
d'ici-bas."

"Son Altesse ma Vanité" frequently tries

to conceal himself.   His voice may be recognised, however, though his features are behind a mask, when he says that his publishers have insisted on the collection of his stories, or that they are issued in response to the earnest solicitation of friends, or in the hope that the work may " be useful in a wider circle," or that they may be " blessed for good," or that they may extend knowledge of the principles for which the gifted and disinterested author is ready to become a second Saint Lawrence if necessary.

No legion of friends have urged upon us the necessity of giving these tales a second chance of immortality—our friends, indeed, are chiefly concerned about their own immortality.   Nor do we look to see the following stories work for good, being quite satisfied with the belief that they will work for no harm.   On the other hand, if the moral is found to be so good that the Board schools will adopt the work for a text-book, we shall be pleased. But there are no principles advocated, because the authors themselves have none.

These tales have all appeared before. "The Case of Mr. Lucraft," which came out as one of a series of short tales in the *World*, has been rewritten, and now contains many additional details of Mr. Lucraft's surprising adventures, which we had to leave out for want of space in the former appearance of the narrative. We venture to present this singular experience as worthy to be compared with that of Peter Schlemyl, the Shadowless. " Titania's Farewell " is based upon certain well-known lines in Hood's " Midsummer Fairies."

Always " son Altesse ma Vanité," and nothing else ? Perhaps not quite. There is one other motive which induces men to write, to publish, to pray for favour at the hands of critics, to hope that subscribers to Smith and Mudie will read and recommend others to read these books. Every man who has a thing to sell, whether it be the offspring of his brain, or something he has bought from others, or something he has planted in the earth and watched while it slowly grew and ripened, will understand what that motive is, and appreciate its force. Perhaps, as a motive influence, it is even stronger than "son Altesse ma Vanité."

W. B. ⎫
J. R. ⎭

PART I.

FROM THE SUPERNATURAL.

THE CASE OF MR. LUCRAFT.

CHAPTER I.

I HAVE more than once told the story of the
only remarkable thing which ever happened
to me in the course of a longish life, but as no
one ever believed me I left off telling it. I
wish, therefore, to leave behind me a truthful record, in which everything shall be set
down, as near as I can remember it, just as it
happened. I am sure I need not add a single
fact. The more I consider the story, the
more I realise to myself my wonderful escape
and the frightful consequences which a providential accident averted from my head,

the more reason I feel to be grateful and humble.

I have read of nothing similar to my own case. I have consulted books on apparitions, witchcraft, and the power of the devil as manifested in authentic history, but I have found absolutely nothing that can in any way compare with my own case. If there be any successor to my Mr. Ebenezer Grumbelow, possessed of his unholy powers, endowed with his fiendish resolve and his diabolical iniquity of selfishness, this plain and simple narrative may serve as a warning to young men situated as I was in the year 1823. Except as a moral example, indeed, I see no use in telling the story at all.

I have never been a rich man, but I was once very poor, and it is of this period that I have to write.

As for my parentage, it was quite obscure. My mother died when I was still a boy ; and my father, who was not a man to be proud of

as a father, had long before run away from
her and disappeared. He was a sailor by
profession, and I have heard it rumoured that
sailors of his time possessed a wife in every
port, besides a few who lived, like my mother,
inland; so that they could vary the sur-
roundings when they wished. The wives
were all properly married in church too, and
honest women, every one of them, What
became of my father I never knew, nor did I
ever inquire.

I went through a pretty fair number of
adventures before I settled down to my first
serious profession. I was travelling com-
panion and drudge to an itinerant tinker, who
treated me as kindly as could be expected
when he was sober. When he was drunk he
used to throw the pots and pans at my head.
Then I became cabin-boy, but only for a
single voyage, on board a collier. The ship
belonged to a philanthropist, who was too
much occupied with the wrongs of the West

Indian niggers to think about the rights of his
own sailors; so his ships, insured far above
their real value, were sent to sea to sink or
swim as it might please Providence. I suppose no cabin-boy ever had so many kicks
and cuffs in a single voyage as I had. However, my ship carried me safely from South
Shields to the port of London. There I ran
away, and I heard afterwards that on her
return voyage the *Spanking Sally* foundered
with all hands. In the minds of those who
knew the captain and his crew personally
there were doubtless, as in mine, grave fears
as to their ultimate destination. After that I
became steward in an Atlantic sailing packet
for a couple of years; then clerk to a bogus
auctioneer in New York; cashier to a store;
all sorts of things, but nothing long. Then I
came back to England, and not knowing
what to do with myself, joined a strolling
company of actors in the general utility line.
It was not exactly promotion, but I liked the

life; I liked the work; I liked the applause; I liked wandering about from town to town; I even liked, being young and a fool, the precarious nature of the salary. Heaven knows mine was small enough; but we were a cheery company, and one or two members subsequently rose to distinction. If we had known any history, which we did not, we might have remembered that Molière himself was once a stroller through France. . Some people think it philosophical to reflect, when they are hard up, how many great men have been hard up too. It would have brought no comfort to me. Practically I felt little inconvenience from poverty, save in the matter of boots. We went share and share alike most of us, and there was always plenty to eat even for my naturally gigantic appetite. Juliet always used to reckon me as equal to four.

Juliet was the manager's daughter—Juliet Kerraus, acting as Miss Juliet Alvanley.

She was eighteen and I was twenty-three, an inflammable and romantic time of life. We were thrown a good deal together too, not only off the stage but on it. I was put into parts to play up to her. I was Romeo when she played her namesake, a part sustained by her mother till even she herself was bound to own that she was too fat to play it any longer ; she was Lady Teazle and I was Charles Surface ; she was Rosalind and I Orlando ; she was Miranda and I Ferdinand ; she was Angelina and I Sir Harry Wildair. We were a pair, and looked well in love scenes. Looking back dispassionately on our performances, I suppose they must have been as bad as stage-acting could well be. At least, we had no training, and nothing but a few fixed rules to guide us ; these of course quite stagey and conventional. Juliet had been on the stage all her life, and did not want in assurance ; I, however, was nervous and uncertain. Then we were badly mounted and badly dressed ; we were ambitious, we ranted, and we tore a passion to rags. But we had one or two good points—we were young and lively. Juliet had the most charming of faces and the most delicious of figures—mind you, in the year 1823 girls had a chance of showing their figures without putting on a page's costume. Then she had a soft sweet voice and pretty little coquettish ways, which came natural to her, and broke through the clumsy stage artificialities. She drew full houses ; wherever we performed all the men, especially all the young officers, used to come after her. They wrote her notes, they lay in wait for her, they sent her flowers ; but what with old Kerrans and myself, to say nothing of the other members of the company, they might as well have tried to get at a Peri in Paradise. I drew pretty well too. I was—a man of seventy and more may say so without being accused of vanity—I was a good-looking young fellow ; you would hardly believe what

quantities of letters and *billets-doux* came to
me. I had dozens, but Juliet found and tore
them all up. There they were ; the note on
rose-coloured note-paper with violet ink,
beginning with "Handsomest and noblest of
men," and ending with "Your fair unknown,
Araminta." There was the letter from the
middle-aged widow with a taste for the drama
and an income; and there was the vilely
spelled note from the foolish little milliner,
who had fallen in love with the Romeo of a
barn. Perhaps ladies are more sensible now.
At all events, their letters were thrown away
upon me, because I was in love already, head
over ears, and with Juliet.

Juliet handed over her notes to her father,
who found out their writers and made them
take boxes and bespeak plays. So that all
Juliet's lovers got was the privilege of paying
more than other people, for the girl was as
good as she was pretty—a rarer combination
of qualities on the stage fifty years ago than

now. She was tall and, in those days, slender. Later on she took after her mother; but who would have thought that so graceful a girl would ever arrive at fourteen stone? Her eyes and hair were black—eyes that never lost their lustre; and hair which, though it turned gray in later years, was then like a silken net, when it was let down, to catch the hearts of lovers. Of course she knew that she was pretty; what pretty woman does not? and of course, too, she did not know and would not understand the power of her own beauty; what pretty woman does? And because it was the very worst thing she could do for herself, she fell in love with me.

Her father knew it, and meant to stop it from the beginning; but he was not a man to do things in a hurry, and so we went on in a fool's paradise, enjoying the stolen kisses and talking of the sweet time to come, when we should be married. One night—I was

Romeo—I was so carried away with passion that I acted for once naturally and unconventionally.   There was a full house ; the performance was so much out of the common, that the people were astonished and forgot to applaud.   Juliet caught the infection of my passion, and for once we acted well, because we acted from the heart.   Never but that once, I believe, has Romeo and Juliet been performed by a pair who felt every word they said.   It was only in a long, low room, a sort of corn exchange or town hall, in a little country town, but the memory of that night is sacred to me.

You know the words—

> "See, how she leans her cheek upon her hand !
> O, that I were a glove upon that hand,
> That I might touch that cheek !"

And these—

> "O, for a falconer's voice,
> To lure this tassel-gentle back again !
> Bondage is hoarse and may not speak aloud,

> Else would I tear the cave where echo lies,
> And make her airy tongue more hoarse than mine
> With repetition of my Romeo !"

Splendidly, we gave them.

Why, even now, old as I am, the recollection of these lines and the thought of that night warm my heart still and fire my feeble pulses. I have taught them to my grandchild. She takes after my poor Juliet, and would succeed on the stage if only her father would let her. But he is straitlaced. Ah! he should have seen the temptations which beset a girl on the stage in my time. We are Puritans now, almost——

And a good thing, too. It is time for me to own it.

Well—old Kerrans was in the front looking after the money, as usual, and always with one eye on the stage, to see how his daughter was getting on. He was puzzled, I think, to make out the meaning of the unaccustomed fire, but he came to the conclusion that if

Juliet was going to remain Miss Juliet, instead of becoming Mrs. Mortimer Vavasseur (my stage name), he had better interfere at once.

So after the play, and over the domestic supper-table, he had it out with his daughter.

Juliet swore that nothing should induce her to marry another man.

" Bless the girl," said her father ; " I don't want you to marry anybody at all."

Juliet declared that she never, never would forget me.

" I don't want you to forget him," Mr. Kerrans replied. " Remember him as much as you like."

Juliet announced her intention of retiring from the stage and going into a convent. There were no convents in England in 1823, so that the threat was not so serious as it would be now.

Her father promised her that when the company passed by any respectable convent on the road, he would certainly knock at the door and inquire about the accommodation and the terms.

"Lor!" he said, caressing his weeping daughter, "do you think I want to be cruel to you, my pretty? Not a bit. Let young Lucraft go and prove himself a man, and he shall have you. But, you see, it wouldn't do to add to the expenses of the company just now, with business so bad and all, would it, my dear? Why, you might be confined in a twelvemonth, and laid by for half the year ever after, with a troop of young children. Where should we be then?"

The next day was Saturday. As usual, I went into the treasury to draw my money, and found the old fellow with rather a red face, and a hesitation in his manner.

He told me the whole story, just as I have told it to you. And then he gave me my dismissal.

"Look here," he said, handing me the

money, "you are a capital young fellow, Lucraft, and a likely actor. There's merit in you. But I can't have you spoiling my Juliet for the stage. So I'm going to put her up without you. After a bit I daresay I shall find another Romeo. You get away to London and find another engagement— there's a week's pay in advance—and when Juliet is married, or when you get rich, or when anything happens to make things different, why, you see, we shall all be glad to see you back. Go and make your fare- wells to Juliet, and don't be more sentimental than you can help. Good-bye, my boy, and good luck to you."

Good luck! Had he known the kind of luck which awaited me!

I sought my girl, and found her crying. I remember that we forgot all the fine verses of Shakespeare, and just put our faces close to each other, and cried together.

It did seem hard upon both of us. We

were really and truly in love, and that in a
good, honest, determined way. To me there
was no other girl in the world except Juliet.
To her' there was no man besides Luke
Lucraft. We had come to an understanding for three months, and had been quietly
dropping deeper and deeper in love during
all that time.

And now we were to part.

" Don't forget me, dear Luke," she sobbed.
" There are lots of prettier and finer girls in
the world than I am, who will try to take
away your love from me. I wish I could
kill the creatures," she added, stamping her
foot.

Juliet always had a high and generous
spirit. · I like women to have a high spirit.

"And will you have no admirers, Juliet ?"
I replied. " Why, half the town "—we were
in Lancaster then—" half the town is at your
feet already. I intercepted two love-letters
yesterday, and I kicked the grocer's appren-

tice the day before for trying to get Mrs. Mould to give you a *billet-doux* from himself. Come, dear, we will trust one another. I will try and prove myself a man—get an engagement, make a name on the London stage, and come back with money and an offer to act Romeo to your Juliet at Drury Lane. Think of that, my dearest, and dry your eyes. Your father does not object to me, you know, he only wants me to make an income. Come, Juliet, let us say good-bye. It is only for a short time, and I shall come back with all sorts of reasons in my pocket for persuading your father's consent."

So we parted, with many more promises of trust and fidelity, and after breaking a sixpenny-bit between us. Juliet's piece is buried with her; mine is hanging at my heart and will be, before long, buried with me beside her.

Oh! the weary journey to London in those days, especially outside the coach, and for

a poor man not encumbered with too many
wraps. However, I arrived at length, and
found myself in the streets that are supposed
to be paved with gold, with a couple of
sovereigns in my pocket.

But I was brimful of hope. London was
a kindly stepmother who received adopted
sons by the thousand, and led them to fame
and wealth. I thought of Garrick, of Dick
Whittington, and all the rest who came up
to town poorer, far poorer than myself, and
took comfort. I secured a lodging at a
modest rent, and made my way to Drury
Lane—the stage door.

I found no opening at Drury Lane ; not
even a vacancy for a supernumerary. There
were not many London theatres in 1823,
and I found the same thing everywhere—
more applications than places to give.

I tried the Greenwich and the Richmond
theatres with the same ill success.

Then I endeavoured to get a country engagement, but I even failed there. I had no friends to recommend me, and my single experience with Kerrans's strolling troupe did not tell so much in my favour as I had hoped.

My ambition naturally took a town flight. I had intended to make my appearance on the metropolitan stage as Romeo, my favourite part, and at once to take the town by storm. I was prepared to give them an intelligent and novel interpretation of Hamlet. And I was not unwilling to undertake Macbeth, Othello, or even Prince Hal.

When these hopes became evidently grounded on nothing but the baseless fabrication of a dream, I resolved on beginning with second parts. Horatio, Mercutio, Paris, were, after all, characters worthy the work of a rising artist.

Again there seemed no chance.

The stage always wants young men of

general utility. I would go anywhere and
take anything. I offered to do so, but
although hopes were held out to me by the
theatrical agent, somehow he had nothing
at the moment in his gift. Nothing : not
even a vacancy for a tragedian at Richard-
son's Show ; not even a chance for Bartholomew Fair.

It took me a fortnight to run down the
scale from Hamlet, say, to Francis the
warder. While I passed through this de-
scending gamut of ambition my two sovereigns were melting away with a rapidity
quite astonishing.

The rent took five shillings. That was
paid in advance. Then I was extravagant in
the matter of eating, and took three meals a
day, finding that not enough to satisfy my
vigorous appetite. Once or twice, too, I
paid for admission to the pit, and saw, with a
sinking heart, what real acting means. My
heart failed, because I perceived that I had

to begin all over again, and from the very bottom of the ladder.

Then I had to buy a new pair of boots. It was always a trouble to me, the rapid wearing out of leather.

And then there was something else ; and then one morning I found myself without a sixpence in my pocket. And then I began for the first time to become seriously alarmed about the future.

I had one or two things which I could pawn—a watch, a waistcoat, a few odds and ends in the way of wardrobe, and a few books—on the proceeds of them I lived for a whole week ; but at last, after spending two-pence in the purchase of a penny loaf and a saveloy for breakfast, I found myself not only penniless, but also without the means of procuring another penny at all, because I had nothing left to pawn.

Many a young fellow has found himself in a similar predicament, but I doubt whether any one ever became so desperately hungry as I did on that day. I recollect that, having rashly eaten up my sausage before eight o'clock, I felt a sinking towards twelve; it was aggravated by the savoury smell of roast meat which steamed from the cook-shops and dining-rooms as I walked along the streets. About one o'clock I gazed with malignant envy on the happy clerks who could go in and order platefuls of the roast and boiled which smoked in the windows, and threw a perfume more delicious than the sweetest strains of music into the streets where I lingered and looked. And at two I observed the diners come out again, walking more slowly, but with an upright and satisfied air, while I—the sinking had been succeeded by a dull gnawing pain—was slowly doubling up. At half-past two I felt as if I could bear it no longer. I had been walking about trying different offices for a clerkship. I might as well have asked for a partnership.

But I could walk no more.   I leaned against a post—it was in Bucklersbury—opposite a dining-room, where hares, fowls, and turkeys were piled in the window among a boundless prodigality and wealth of carrots, turnips, and cauliflowers, till my senses swam at the contemplation.   I longed for a caldron in which to put the whole contents of the shop front, and eat them at one Gargantuan repast.   My appetite, already alluded to, was hereditary; one of the few things I can remember of my mother was a constant complaint that my father used to eat her out of house and home.   To be sure, from other scraps of information handed down by tradition, I have reason to believe that the word eating was used by a figure of speech—the part for the whole—and included drinking. I was good at both, and as a trencherman I had been unsurpassed, as I said above, in the company, the dear old company among whom I have so often eaten beefsteak and fried onions with Juliet. The door of the place opened now and then to let a hungry man enter or a full man go out, and I caught a glimpse of the interior. Dining-rooms were not called restaurants in those days. They had no gilding, no bright paint, no pretty barmaids, and no silver-plated forks and spoons. Nor were they brilliant with gas. All London—that is, all working London— dined before four o'clock; the clerks from twelve to two, and the principals, except a few of the big wigs, from two to four. The cheaper rooms were like one or two places still to be found in Fleet Street. There were sanded floors ; there were hard benches, you had your beer out of pewter, not plated tankards ; there was no cheap claret, and the popular ideal of wine was a strong and fiery port. Also, candles stood upon the tables—not wax candles, but tallow, with long wicks which required snuffing. They dropped a good deal of mutton fat about the

table, and it was not uncommon to find yourself eating a little tallow with your bread,
which was not nice even to men of a strong
stomach.   Finally, you had steel forks, which
are just as good, to my thinking, as plated
silver, and more easily cleaned.

I stood by the post and watched with
hungry eyes.   From within I heard voices,
stifled voices, as those sent up a pipe,
calling for roast beef with plenty of brown
—good heavens! plenty of brown; roast
mutton, underdone — I loved my mutton
underdone; boiled beef with suet-pudding
and fat — I always took a great deal of
pudding and fat with my boiled beef; roast
veal and bacon with stuffing—a dish for the
gods; calves' head for two—I could have
eaten calves' head for a dozen; with orders
pointing to things beyond my hungry
imagination — hunger limits the boundaries
of fancy—puddings; fish, soup, cheese, and
such delicacies.   Alas! I wanted the solids.

I felt myself growing feebler; I became more and more doubled up; I had thoughts of entering this paradise of the hungry, and, after eating till I could eat no longer, calmly laying down my knife and fork and informing the waiter that I had no money. There was a farce in which I had once played where the comic actor sent for the landlord, after a hearty meal, and asked him what he would do in case a stranger after ordering and eating his dinner should declare his inability to pay. " Do, sir ? " cried the host, " I should kick him across the street." "Landlord," said the low-comedian, and it always told,—" Landlord," he used to rise up slowly as he spoke, and solemnly draw aside his coat-tails, turning his face in the direction of the street-door, —" landlord, I'll trouble you." I used to play the landlord.

It struck half-past three; the dead gnawing of hunger was followed by a sharp pain, irritating and much more unpleasant. The crowd of those who entered had been followed by the crowd of those who came out, and the heaven of hungry men was nearly empty again. I gazed still upon the turkeys and the hares, but with a lack-lustre eye, for I was nearly fainting.

Presently there came down the street an elderly gentleman, bearing before him, like a Lord Mayor in a French tale, his enormous abdomen : he had white hair, white eyebrows, white whiskers, and a purple face. He walked very slowly, as if the exertion might prove apoplectic, and leaned upon a thick stick. As he passed the shop he looked in at the window and wagged his head. At that moment I groaned involuntarily. He turned round and surveyed me. I suppose I presented a strange appearance, leaning against the post, with stooping figure and tightly buttoned coat. He had big projecting eyes flushed with red veins, which gave him a wolfish expression.

" Young man," he said, not benignantly at all, but severely, " you look ill. Have you been drinking ? "

I shook my head.

" I am only hungry," I said ; telling the truth because I was really too far gone to hide it—" I am only hungry; that is the matter with me."

He planted his stick on the ground, supporting both his hands upon the gold head, and wagged his head again from side to side with a grunting sound in his throat like the sawing of bones.

Grunt ! " Here's a pretty fellow for you ! " Grunt ! " Hungry, and he looks miserable." Grunt ! " Hungry, and he groans." Grunt ! " Hungry — the most enviable condition a man can be in—and he dares to repine at his lot." Grunt ! "What are the lower classes coming to next, I wonder. Aren't you ashamed of yourself ? Aren't you a model of everything that is ungrateful and "—

grunt!—"and flying in the face of Providence?   He lives in a land of victuals.
London is a gigantic caravan, full of the most
splendid things, the most glorious things to
eat and drink; it only wants an appetite;
and he's got that, and he laments!"

"What is the use of an appetite if you
have no money to satisfy it with?"

Grunt!   "Is it a small appetite, as a rule,
or is it a large appetite?"

"Large," I replied.   "It is an awkward
thing for a poor beggar like me to have such
a devil of a twist.   I was born with it.
Very awkward just now."

"Come with me, young man," he grunted.
"Go before me.   Don't talk, because that
may interfere with the further growth of
your appetite.   Walk slowly and keep your
mouth shut close."

He came behind me, walking with his
chuckle and grunt.

"So.   What a fine young fellow it is!"

Grunt! "What room for the development of the Alderman's Arch! What a back-bone for the support of a stomach! What shoulders for a dinner-table, and what legs to put under it! Heavens! what a diner might be made of this boy if he only had money." Grunt! "Youth and appetite—health and hunger — and all thrown away upon a pauper! What a thing, what a thing! This way, young man."

Turning down a court leading out of Bucklersbury he guided me to a door, a little black portal, at which he stopped; then stooping to a keyhole of smaller size than was generally used in those days, he seemed to me to blow into it with his mouth; this was absurd, of course, but it seemed so to me. The door opened. He led the way into a passage which, when the door shut behind us, as it did of its own accord, was pitch dark. We went up some stairs, and on the first landing the old gentleman, who was wheezing and puffing tremendously, opened another door, and led me into a room. It was a large room, resplendent with the light of at least forty wax candles. The centre was occupied by a large dining-table laid for a single person. Outside it was broad daylight, for it was not yet four o'clock.

"Sit down, young man, sit down," puffed my host. "Oh dear! oh dear! Sit down, do. I wish I was as hungry as you."

I sat down in the nearest chair, and looked round the room. The first thing I remarked was that I could not see the door by which we had been admitted. The room was octa-gonal, and on every side stood some heavy piece of furniture: a table with glass, a case of bookshelves, a sofa, but no door. My head began to go round as I continued my observations. There was no window either, nor was there any fireplace. Then I felt a sudden giddiness, and I suppose I fell back-

wards on my chair. It was partly the faintness of hunger, but partly it was the strange
room, and that old man glaring at me with
his great wolfish eyes.

When I recovered I was lying on a sofa,
and soft cold fingers were bathing my head,
and pressing a perfumed handkerchief to my
lips. I opened my eyes suddenly and sat up
completely recovered. At the foot of the
sofa stood my entertainer.

" Easy with him, Boule-de-neige ; make
him rest for a moment. Perhaps his hunger
has been too much for him."

I turned to see who Boule-de-neige was.
He was a negro of the blackest type, as
ancient and withered as some old ourang of
tropical woods ; his cheeks hung in folds, and
his skin seemed too much for his attenuated
body ; his wool was white, and his gums were
almost toothless ; and his nose so flattened
with age as to be almost invisible, looking at
him as I was looking, in profile. His hands

were as soft as any woman's, but icy cold ;
and his eyes were red and fiery.

"Boule-de-neige, what do you think of
him ?"

"Him berry fine young man, massa : him
beautiful young man ; got lubly abbatite
develoffed, I tink ; him last long time, much
longer time dan last oder young man. Cluck!
Him poor trash, dat young man ; dam poor
trash ; use up and go to de debbel in a
month. Cluck! Dis young man got lubly
stumjack, strong as bull. Cluck-cluck! How
much you tink him eat to night ?"

"We shall see; Boule-de-neige. We will
try him with a simple dinner, and then pro-
nounce on his performances. Young men do
not always come up to their professions. But
he looks well, and perhaps, Boule-de-neige—
perhaps—ah !" He nodded with a deep
sigh.

"What time massa dine himself ?"

"I don't know," the old gentleman answered, with another heavy sigh. " Perhaps not till nine o'clock ; perhaps not then. It all depends on this youth. Vanish, Boule-de-neige, and serve."

There was evidently something in my host's mind by the way he sighed. Why did it depend upon me ? And did Boule-de-neige go through the floor ? Did the table sink when he disappeared, and come up loaded with dishes ? It seemed so.

I sprang from the couch. The sight and smell of the food brought back my raging hunger.

" Let me eat ! " I cried.

" You shall. One moment first—only a single moment. Young man, tell me again and explicitly the nature and extent of your appetite. Be truthful ; oh, be truthful ! Our little tongues should never lie for mutton-chop or apple-pie. You know the hymn. I hope you have been religiously brought up, and know that hymn."

" I've got a devil of an appetite. What is there to lie about ? "

" My dear young friend, there are many kinds of appetites. Yours may be fierce at first and promise great things, and then end in a miserably small performance. I have known such, and mourned to see them. Is it a lasting appetite, now ? Is it steady through a long dinner ? Is it regular in its recurrence ? "

" You shall see something of my performance," I laughed, insensate wretch. " You shall see. I never had a long dinner in my life, because I always make short work of mine. It is steady through a good many pounds of steak, and as regular as a clock."

" That is, always something. Steak is as healthy a test as I know. Is it, secondly, an appetite that recovers itself quickly ? That is very important. Is it a day-by-day or an hour-by-hour appetite ? Is it good at all times of the day ? "

" Alas, I wish it were not ! "

" Hush, young man; do not blaspheme !
Tell me, if you eat your fill now—it is half-
past four—when do you think you might
be ready again ? " His eyes glistened like a
couple of great rubies in the candlelight, and
his hands trembled.

" I should say about eight. But I might
do something light at seven, I daresay. Just
now I feel as if I could eat a mountain."

" He feels as if he could eat a mountain !
Wonderful are the gifts of Providence ! My
dear young friend, I am very thankful—
deeply thankful—that I met you. Sit down
and let me take the covers off for you ; I
long to see you eat. This is a blessed
day—a truly blessed day ! I will wait upon
you myself. No one else. Boule-de-neige,
vanish ! "

As he was about to take off the covers he
stopped short.

" Stay. You are without occupation ? "

" I can get none."

" You are of any trade ? "

" I am an actor."

" A bad trade—an un-Christian trade. Actors are vagabonds by act of parliament. Actors can never be in a state of grace. I shall be happy in being a humble instrument in removing you from a calling fatal to the Christian warrior. Why did you leave your last situation ? No dishonesty ? No embezzlement ? No tampering with accounts ? "

" Sir, I have always been an honest man. And, besides, I have never been tempted by the handling of other people's money."

" Ha ! You have got no wife ? "

" No, sir ; I am unmarried."

" You have got no—— I trust I am taking to my bosom no deceiver of women. You are not the father of an illegitimate offspring, I hope and pray."

" No, sir ; I am not."

" Young man, you are about to enter upon a most serious act, perhaps the most serious act of your life, and these questions may appear to you trivial and tedious. As a Christian, and a member of the congregation of Mr. —— But never mind ; you are hungry now, and wish to eat. We will talk after dinner."

He took off the covers. The table was spread with a dozen different dishes, all served up together. Others I noticed, standing with bottles· and decanters, on a large sideboard. As my generous benefactor removed the silver covers, his face, which had assumed during his questioning an austere gravity, suddenly lit up, and he laughed aloud as the perfume of the hot food mounted to his nostrils. He seemed all at once a different man.

"Gently, gently, my dear young friend. Here is a dinner fit for a king ; fit for *me*, if I could eat it. Oh ! my dainty Boule-de-neige! Ha! is it right to waste such a dinner upon a youth whose only dreams are of a sufficiency of steak? Young man, in after years—ahem!—in after days you will remember this dinner. You will recall every item in this most delicious bill of fare which Boule-de-neige has set before you. Let me teach you to eat it properly. Weigh your morsels."

Heaven! how I cursed his delay. He kept one great hand between me and the dishes, for fear, I suppose, that I should pounce upon them and clear them off all at once.

"Patience, patience. Consider each mouthful. Try to be thankful that cooks have brought their divine art to such perfection. Carry back your thoughts to—grunt—to time when all mankind fed upon imperfectly cooked steak. Think that all the treasures of the East and West have been ransacked to furnish for me this meal, and that you will never, never, never see such a dinner again as long as you live."

At all events I never saw such a meal again as long as *he* lived.

"We will now," he said, with a backward wave of his right hand, "consider dinner as a science."

"Oh, sir!" I exclaimed, "I am so hungry."

"It's beautiful to see you hungry, but I must not let you hurry. Eat as much as you like when you begin, but gently, gently— easily and gently. Think of the future. Think of ME."

I stared at him in wonder.

"Think of you, sir?"

"Why, what would happen to me if you really destroyed your appetite, or even yourself in swallowing a bone?"

I thought he must be mad.

"Young man," he went on. "You will say a grace before meat, if you remember one."

I did not.

"Then I will say one for you. Oh! wretched trade of stage acting. He does not even know a single grace before meat."

Then he began to help me—and we went on with dinner without further interruption. He kept up a running accompaniment of comment as I devoured the meal, and his manner gradually lost all its solemnity, until before I was more than half through the dinner he was dancing about, slapping his leg with delight, and laughing till he grew almost black in the face.

Why he was so pleased I could not tell. I was soon to learn.

"These are plovers' eggs. No better thing ever discovered to begin your dinner with. Alderman Stowport says oysters are better. That is rubbish. I do not despise oysters—Why, he has eaten the whole six! Bravo! bravo! an excellent beginning. Let me take away the plate, my dear sir. Now

we have turtle soup — gently, my young
friend, gently. Ah, impetuous youth!
More? Stay—green fat. Humour, humour
your appetite; don't drive it; calipash and
calipee. It's really sinful to eat so fast. He
takes all down without tasting it. No—no
more; you must give yourself a fair chance
and not spoil your dinner with too much
turtle." He put the soup aside, and took
the cover off another dish. "Salmon—with
cucumber. Lobster-sauce—bless me, it's like
a dream of fairyland! Fillet of sole—a beautiful dream to see him. Ho! ho! he's a Julius
Cæsar the Conqueror. Croquet de volaille—
gone like a cloud from the sky. Don't wolf
the food, my friend; there is a limit to the
cravings of nature imposed by the claims of
art; taste it. Ris de veau—smiles of the
dear little innocent, confiding calf—a little
more bread with it? Mauviettes en caisse,
larks in baskets—sweet, rapturous, singing
larks, toothsome cockyolly larks. He eats

them up, bones and all. Ha! ha! Pause,
my dear sir, and drink something.   Here are
champagne, hock, and sauterne ; never touch
sherry, it's a made-up wine, even the best of
it.   Come, a little champagne."

"I generally take draught-beer, sir," I
replied modestly.   " That is the drink to
which I have been accustomed and—not too
much of it ; but, if you please, a little fizz will
be acceptable."

I drank three glasses in rapid succession,
and found them good.   He meanwhile
nodded and winked with an ever-increasing
delight which I failed to understand.

" Now, my Nero, my Paris of Troy, my
Judas Maccabæus "—he mixed up his names,
but it mattered nothing—" here is saddle of
mutton, with potatoes, cauliflower, currant-
jelly. More champagne ?   It's worth *sums*
of money to see him. Curry ? More champagne ? Curry of chicken ? Cabob curry
of chicken, young Alexander the Great ?

Plenty of rice? Ho, ho, ho! Plenty of rice, he said; why, he is a Goliath—a Goliath of Gath, this young man!"

He really grew so purple that I thought he would have a fit of some kind. But the flattery pleased me all the same, and I went on eating and drinking as if I was only just beginning.

"Quail or bécassine—snipe, that is? He takes both, like Pompey. More champagne? Jelly, my Heliogabalus, my modern Caracalla, apricot-jelly? Cabinet pudding? He has two helpings of the pudding. King Solomon in all his 'glory never—— More champagne? A little hock to finish with? He takes his hock in a tumbler, this young Samson. Cheese—Brie—and celery. A glass of port with the cheese. He takes that in a tumbler too, like Og, King of Bashan."

I was really overwhelmed with the splendour of the dinner, the classical and biblical flattery, and the extraordinary gratification

which my really enormous hunger caused
this remarkable old gentleman. He clapped
his hands ; he nodded his head ; he slapped
his legs ; he winked and grinned ; he smacked
his lips ; he evinced every sign of the most
unbounded delight. When I had quite
finished eating, which was not before we
had got through the whole list of courses,
he gave me a bottle of claret, and watched
me while I rapidly disposed of it. Then he
produced from a sideboard, where I certainly
had not seen it a moment before, a small cup
of strong black coffee with a tiny glass of
liqueur. As for my own part, I hope I have
made it clear that I dined extremely well ; in
fact, I had never even dreamed of such a
dinner in my life. It was not only that I was
half starved, but that the things were so
good. Imagine the astonishment of a young
strolling actor, whose highest dreams were
of sufficient beefsteak, not of the primest
part, at such a magnificent feed. I felt as

if I had dropped unexpectedly into a fortune.
I had.

" How do you feel now ? " my host asked,
a shade of anxiety crossing his brow.

CHAPTER II.

THERE was still the strange look in my host's eyes—a sort of passionate and eager longing.

"I am very well, thank you, sir, and more grateful than I can tell you."

" Hang the gratitude! Tell me if you feel any sense of repletion ? Does the blood seem mounting to the head ? Are you quite free from any giddiness ? No thickness in the speech ? It's wonderful, it's providential, my finding you. Such a windfall; and just when I most wanted it. Our blessings truly come when we least expect them."

This was strange language, but the whole proceedings were so strange that I hardly

noticed it. Besides, I was extremely comfortable after my dinner, and disposed to rest.

"Now," he went on, "while you are digesting—by the way, the digestion is, I trust,
unimpaired by drink or excess? Quite so;
and what I expected in so good and so gifted
a young man. Like an ostrich, as you say.
Ho, ho! ha, ha! like an ostrich! It is, indeed,
too much. Tell me, now, something, gently
and dispassionately, so as not to injure your
digestion, about your history."

I told him all. While I related my simple
story he interrupted now and then with some
fresh question on the growth, the endurance,
the regularity of my appetite, to which I gave
satisfactory answers. When I had quite
finished he went to the table—I noticed then
that all traces of the dinner had disappeared
—and laid out a document, by which he
placed a pen. Then he drew a chair, sat
down in front of me, and assumed a serious
air.

" Come," he said peremptorily, "let us get now to business."

I had not the smallest notion what the business was but I bowed and waited. Perhaps he was going to offer me a clerkship. Visions of a large salary, to suit my expansive appetite, came across my brain.

" In your case," he began, " the possession of so great an appetite must be attended with serious inconveniences. You have no money; in a few hours you will be hungry again; you will endure great pain and suffering, greater than is felt by men less largely endowed with the greatest blessing—I mean with appetite."

" Yes," I said, " it is a great trouble to me this twist of mine, especially when I am hard up."

He almost jumped out of his chair.

" Why, there," he cried, "what is the use of words ? We are agreed already. Nothing could be more fortunate. Let us have no more beating about the bush. Young man, I

will rid you of this nuisance ; I will buy your
appetite of you."

I only stared. Was the old gentleman
mad ?

" It is a strange offer, I know," he went
on, " a strange offer, and you have probably
never heard a more remarkable one. But
it is genuine. I will buy your appetite of
you."

" Buy my—buy my appetite ? "

" Nothing easier.   Read this."

He gave me the paper which he had laid
on the table, prepared in readiness, I suppose,
for me.   It was as follows :

" I, Luke Lucraft, being in sound mind and
in good health, and of the mature age of
twenty-four, do voluntarily and of my own
free will and accord agree and promise to
resign my appetite entirely and altogether for
the use of Ebenezer Grumbelow from the
day and hour of the execution of this deed.
In return whereof I agree to accept a monthly

allowance of £30, also to date from the moment of signature, with a sum of £50, to be placed in my hands.   I promise also that I will carefully study to preserve by regular habits and exercise the gift of a generous appetite ; that I will not work immoderately, sit up late, practise vicious courses, or do anything that may tend to impair the regular recurrence of a healthy and vigorous hunger."

Then followed a place for the signature and one for the witnesses.

"You see," he went on, "I ask for no unpleasant condition.   I give you a free life, coupled with the simple condition of ordinary care.   Do you agree ? "

" I hardly know ; it is so sudden."

" Come, come "—he spoke with a harshness quite new—" come, let us have no nonsense of that sort.   Do you agree ? "

I read it over again.

" Give me a little time," I said.   " Let me reflect till to-morrow morning."

"Reflect!" his face flushed purple, and his
bloodshot eyes literally glared. "Reflect!
what the devil does the boy want to reflect
about? Has he got a penny, a friend, or a
chance in the whole world? I will give you
five minutes—come." He rose up and stood
before me. As I looked in his face a curious
dimness came over my eyes; he seemed to
recede before me; he disappeared altogether.
When I heard him speak again his voice
sounded far, far off, but thin and clear, as if
it came through some long tube. "Luke
Lucraft," it said, "see yourself."

Yes; I saw myself, and though *outside* of
what I saw, I felt the same emotions as if I
had been the actual performer in the scenes I
witnessed.

I was standing where the old gentleman
met me, starving still, and suffering pangs far
worse than those under which I groaned at
three o'clock. The day was advanced; the
diners had all gone away, and the dining-

room waiters were putting up the shutters.
I spoke to one of them timidly.   I told him
I had eaten nothing since the morning, and
begged for a plate of broken victuals.   He
looked in my face, called a brother servant,
and they kicked me from the door.   People
were rougher in London fifty years ago.
Then I slunk away, and wandered some-
where among the winding streets and lanes
of the old city.   London at night was not so
empty and deserted as it is now, and the
streets had people in them.   Some of them
were well dressed—the wealthy merchants
had not, even then, all left off living in the
city; some were clerks going home; some
were women out for an evening's walk.   The
bells rang out the hours from the city clocks,
and I crept along the walls wondering what
would become of me, and how I should find
an end of my present misery.

Then I begged.   Took off my hat and
held it in my hand while I asked for some-

thing—anything—the smallest coin that would get a piece of bread.

The men passed me by with pitiless and un-believing eyes. Heavens! if they had been hungry once, only once, in all their lives, they would never again have refused the petition of a beggar, even though he was the most lying mendicant who ever disgraced the words of charity which passed his lips. But they gave me nothing.

The women edged away from me and passed on the other side if I timidly pressed my claim. They had nothing to fear from me. At last I asked a girl. She was more unfortunate than myself, but she was not hungry, and she gave me a shilling.

Then I found a shop open, and bought a plate of meat. That spent—I saw myself slinking, ashamed and wretched, again along the cold and empty streets. When I could walk no more I found myself in Covent Garden Market, and threw myself under shelter of a roof at least, among the stalks and leaves and straw which littered the place.

I awoke early, and hungry again. I rose and resumed my miserable walk.

Hope by this time was dead within me; I could think of nothing but my intolerable hunger; could feel nothing but the pain which would not leave me; could look at nothing but food in the window.

I begged again and begged all day without success.

It was a rougher time, that, than the present. More than one man laid his stick across my back with an impatient admonition to get to work, you lazy rogue. But I was too feeble to retaliate or to remonstrate. Was there no charity in the world? I passed other beggars in the streets who looked fat and comfortable. People gave *them* money, but they would give me none. The time wore on and my craving for food became irresistible.

I passed a shop which had a tray outside
of baked potatoes. The owner had his back
to me. I *stole* one. Yes, I stole one. No
one saw me. He did not see me as I slunk
past him with guilty face, and swiftly sped
round the nearest corner to eat the stolen
morsel.

What is the use of a single baked potato ?
Presently I returned to the same place with
the intention of taking another. But they
were all gone. I went on looking for another
provision shop. I came to a place where hot
smoking sausages were bubbling in a pan
over a charcoal fire. The shop stood at a
corner. There was only a girl minding it.
I deliberately walked in, took a sausage from
the pan, hot as it was, and stepped out again
before her astonishment even prompted her
to cry out.

The time seemed intolerably long. All
these scenes passed before me, not as the
quick and steady flight of the rapidly falling

moments, but as if the agony and the shame were deliberately lengthened out.

Then came a third time when I stole, maddened by the dream of hunger. This time I was detected, pursued, and apprehended. The misery and shame of the hour when I stood before the magistrate, in that horrible vision of a possible future, I cannot even yet forget. With this a constant sense of unsatisfied and craving hunger; a feeling as if hunger was the greatest evil in the whole world; a longing to get rid of it. Last scene of all, I was lying dead, starved to death with hunger and cold, in a miserable, bare, and naked garret.

By what black art did the old man delude my senses? It was a lie, and he knew it. I should have got some honest work, if only to wheel bricks or carry loads.

" There is your future, young man "—there came up from the distance the voice of the tempter—" a gloomy prospect: a miserable

life : a wretched ending.   Now look at the
other side."

The scene changed.   I saw myself, but in
another guise.   My hunger had vanished ; I
felt it no more.

This time I was happy, light-hearted, and
cheerful.   I remembered scenes of misery
through which I had just passed, and the
recollection added more sweetness to my
present enjoyment.   It seemed as if I should
never be hungry any more, and never feel
the want of food.   I was like a Greek god
in my exemption from the common weakness
of humanity.   I was rich, too, and knew that
I had the command, somehow, of all that
money could buy.

I was sitting in a garden, and around me
were troops of girls.   I heard the rustle of
their dresses, caught the laughter from their
lips, watched the lustre of their eyes, saw
the moonlight dance among their waving
locks as they ran and played among the

trees and flowers. One of them sat by me
and sang to a guitar—

> Life is made for love. Ah! why
>   Should its sweetness e'er be marred?
> List! the echoes will not die,
>   Still the sweet word "love" to guard.
>
> Nought but love. Oh! happy youth
>   Free from need of baser thought,
> Stay with us, and learn this truth,
>   Set with song, with music wrought.
>
> Thine is love, an endless feast;
>   Beauty—sweeter far than wine;
> Joy, from lower cares released—
>   Never star rose bright as thine.

I knew, somehow or other, that this was
allegorical, and, as if I expressed my thought,
the scene changed, and I was in real life.

Chambers in London, such as I had read
of, overlooking St. James's Park. I sat
in them in the midst of books and pictures.
I had no business to call me away from my
indolent ease; I had no anxiety about the
future. I got up and strolled about the

streets looking at the shops. If I fancied a
thing I bought it.   I went to picture galleries
and saw the latest works of art.   I went to
the theatre, and saw the performance from a
comfortable box : I went riding in the park.

Then my fancy returned to my first love,
and I saw myself walking in a country lane
with Juliet.   She was sweeter to look upon
than ever, and more delightful in her frank
and innocent love for me.   We rambled along
under the hedges while I gathered flowers
for her, and talked of the happy, happy days
when we should be one, soon now to arrive,
and of the sweet, loving life which should
be ours far away from the troubles of the
world.

Dreams ; idle dreams ; but sweet to me,
after the agony of the last, as a draught of
water to a parched traveller on Sahara.

The pictures changed as fast as my fancy
wandered from one thing to another.   In all I
was the same—free from the downward and

earthly pressure of want and hunger, relieved from anxiety, with plenty of money, and full of all sweet and innocent fancies.

Lies again. But by what power could this necromancer so cheat and gull my brain?

"Very different scenes these, my dear young friend," he said in a winning voice, "are they not? Now," he went on, and his voice was quite close to me, "you have had your five minutes."

The cloud passed from my eyes. I was sitting again in the octagonal room, the old man before me, watch in hand, as if he was counting the seconds.

"Five minutes and a quarter," he growled. "Now choose."

"I have chosen," I replied. "I accept your offer."

The influence of the things I had seen was too strong upon me. I could neither reason nor reflect.

"I accept your offer."

"Why, that's brave," he said, with a gigantic sigh of relief. "That's what I expected of you. Boule-de-neige—Boule-de-neige!"

He clapped his hands.

Instantly the horrible old negro appeared behind his master's chair, as if he had sprung up from the ground. I believe he had. He looked more like a devil than ever, grinning from ear to ear, and his two eyes glowing in the candlelight like two great coals. The light fell too upon the seams and wrinkles of his face, bringing them out like the hills and valleys in a raised map. Strange as it all was to me, this ancient servitor produced the strangest effect upon me of anything.

" Boule-de-neige is witness for us," said the old gentleman. " Boule-de-neige, this young gentleman, Mr. Luke Lucraft, is about to sign a little deed, to which, as a matter of form, we require your signature too as witness."

"Cluck!" said the negro. "Dis young gegleman berry lucky—him berry lucky. What time massa take him dinner?"

"When do you think you shall be fairly hungry again?" he asked me. "Now, no boastings—no false pretence and pride—because it will be the worse for you. Answer truthfully. It is now six."

"I should say that at nine I should be able to take some supper, and at ten I shall certainly be hungry again. As an ordinary rule I should be ready a great deal earlier, but I have taken such an immense dinner."

"Good." He turned to Boule-de-neige. "You see, the young man is modest and promises fairly. I shall have supper—a plentiful supper—at ten punctually. Mr. Lucraft will now sign."

I advanced to the table and took up the pen, but there was no ink.

"Cluck!" said the infernal negro with another grin—"cluck! Massa wait lilly bit."

He took my left hand in his soft and cold paw. I felt a sharp prick at my wrist.

"You will dip the pen," said the old gentleman, "in the blood. It is a mere form."

"Cluck!" said Boule-de-neige.

"A mere form, because we have no ink handy."

"Cluck-cluck!"

I signed my name as desired and, following the directions of the old gentleman, placed my finger on the red wafer at the margin, saying, "I declare this my act and deed."

Then I gave the pen to Boule-de-neige. He signed after me in a firm flowing hand, "Boule-de-neige." As I looked, the letters seemed somehow to shape themselves into "Beelzebub." I looked at him with a kind of terror. The creature grinned in my face as if he divined my thought, and gave utterance to one of his hideous "clucks."

Then I began to feel the same faintness

which I had at first experienced. It mounted upwards from my feet slowly, so that I heard the old gentleman's voice, though I saw nothing. It grew gradually fainter.

" Supper at ten, Boule-de-neige," he was saying; " I feel getting hungry already. What shall I do with myself till ten o'clock ? I am certainly getting hungry. I think I can have it served at half-past nine. O, blessed day! O, thankful, blessed day! Boule-de-neige, it must be supper for three—for four—for five. I shall have champagne—the Perrier Jouet—the curaçoa punch afterwards. Curaçoa punch—I haven't tasted it for three months and more. Oh, what a blessed— blessed—blessed——"

I heard no more because my senses failed me altogether, and his voice died away in my ears.

When I came to myself I was leaning against the post in Bucklersbury, where I had met the old man.

A whiff of stale cooked meat from the
cook-shop, which caught me as I opened my
eyes, produced a singular feeling of disgust.
"Pah," I muttered, "roast mutton!" and
moved from the spot. My hunger was gone,
that was quite certain. I felt a quietness
about those regions, wherever they may be,
which belong to appetite. I was almost
dreamy in the repose which followed a
morning so stormy. I walked quietly away
homewards in a kind of daze, trying to make
out something of what had happened. The
first thing I found I could not remember was
the name of the old gentleman. When that
came back to me and under what circumstances I will tell you as we get along. Bit
by bit I recalled the whole events of the
afternoon, one after the other. I saw the old
man, with his purple face and bloodshot eyes
and white hair; I saw the wrinkled and
seamed old negro; I saw the octagonal room
without doors or windows; the splendid

dinner; the host watching my every gesture; I remembered everything except the name of the man to whom I had sold—my appetite.

.It was so strange that I laughed when I thought of it. I must have been drunk: he gave me a good dinner and I took too much wine; but, then, how was it that I remembered clearly every, even the smallest, detail?

On the bed in the one room which constituted my lodging I found a letter. It was from a firm of lawyers, dated that evening at half-past six—only half an hour after I signed the paper—stating that they were empowered by a client, whose name was not mentioned, to give me the sum of £30 monthly, to begin from that day, and to be paid to me personally. How did they get their instructions, then? And it was all true!

I was too tired with the day's adventures to think any more; and though it was only nine o'clock I went to bed and fell fast asleep. In an hour I awoke again, with a choking

sensation, as if I was eating too much. I
knew instantly what was going on, and by
a kind of prophetic insight. The old man
was taking his supper, and taking more than
was good—*for me*. I sprang from the bed
gasping for breath. Presently, as I gathered,
he began to drink too much as well. My
brain went round and round. I laughed,
sang, and danced; and soon after, with a
heavy fall, I rolled senseless on the carpet,
and remembered nothing more.

It was early in the morning when I awoke,
still lying on the floor. I had a splitting
headache. I had fallen against some corner
of the furniture and blackened one eye. I
had broken two chairs somehow or other. I
was cold, ill, and shaken. I got into bed,
and tried to remember what had happened.
Clearly I must have made a drunken beast of
myself over the dinner, and reeled home with
my head full of fancies and dreams; perhaps
the dinner itself was a dream and a halluci-

nation too ; if so, the pangs of hunger would soon recommence. But they did not. Then I fell asleep, and did not awake again till the clock struck twelve. How ill and wretched I felt as I dressed! My hand shook, my eyes were red, my face swollen. Surely I must have been intoxicated. I had been, up to that day at least, a temperate man, partly no doubt from the very wholesome reason which keeps so many of us sober—the necessity of poverty ; but of course I had not arrived at four and twenty years and seen so much of the world without recognising the signs of too much drink. I had them, every one ; and, as most men know too well, they are all summed up in the simple expression, "hot coppers." Alas! I was destined to become only too, familiar with the accursed symptoms. Involuntarily, when I had dressed myself, I put my hands in my pockets, those pockets so often empty ; there was money, gold—sovereigns—my pocket was full of them. I

counted them in a stupor. Forty-nine, and
one rolled into the corner—fifty ; it was part
of the sum for which I had sold my appetite ;
and on the table lay the letter from Messrs.
Crackett & Charges, inviting me to draw
thirty pounds a month.

Then it was all true !

I sat down and, with my throbbing temples
and feverish pulse, tried to make it out.
Everything became plain except the name of
the purchaser—Mr.—Mr.—— I remembered
Boule-de-neige, the house, the room, and the
dinner, but not the name of that arch-deceiver,
the whole of whose villany I was far from
realising yet; and until it was told me later on
I never did remember the name.

It was strange. Men are said to have sold
their souls to the devil for money, bartering
away an eternity of happiness for a few years
of pleasure ; but as for me I had exchanged,
as it seemed at first sight, nothing but the
inconvenience of a healthy appetite with

nothing to eat for the means of living comfortably without it. There could be no sin in
such a transaction ; it was on a different level
altogether from the bargain made by Faust.
And there were the broad, the benevolent
facts, so to speak—my pocket full of sovereigns, and the letter instructing me to call
at an office for thirty pounds monthly.

Benevolent facts I thought them. You
shall see. You think, as I thought, that no
sin could be laid to my door for the
transaction. You shall judge. You think, as
I thought, that no harm could follow so simple
a piece of business. You shall read. On my
way out I met the landlady, who gave me
notice to quit at the end of the week.

" I thought you were a quiet and a sober
young man," she said. " Ah, never will I
trust to good looks again. Me and the
lodgers kept awake till two in the morning
with your singing and dancing, let alone
banging the floor with the chairs. Not

another hour after your week's up, if you was
to pray on your knees, shall you stay.   And
next door threatening the constables; and
me a quiet woman for twenty years."

My heart sank again.   But after all, perhaps it was I myself, not the good old
gentleman, my kind patron and benefactor, at
all, who was the cause of this disturbance.
It was undoubtedly true that I had taken a
great quantity of wine with my splendid
dinner.   I begged her pardon humbly, and
passed out.

It was now nearly one o'clock, but I felt no
desire for breakfast.   That was an experience
quite novel to me.   Still I went to a coffee-
house, according to habit, and ordered some
tea and a rasher. When they came I discovered, with a horrid foreboding of worse
misfortune behind, that my taste was gone.
Except that one thing was solid and the other
liquid, I distinguished nothing.   Nor did my
sense of smell assist me ; as I found later, my

nose was affected agreeably or disagreeably, but it lost all its discriminating and critical powers. Gunpowder, sulphuretted hydrogen gas, and tobacco offended my nose. So did certain smells belonging to cookery. On the other hand, certain flowers, tea, and claret pleased me, but I was unable to distinguish between them. Not only could I not taste things, but I had no gratification in eating them. I ate and drank mechanically, because I knew that the body must be kept going on something.

All this knowledge, however, and more, came by degrees. After making a forced breakfast I bent my steps to the lawyers', who had an office in Lincoln's-inn Fields.

The letter was received by a conceited young clerk in shiny black habiliments, a turned up nose, and a self-satisfied manner.

" Ha!" he said, " I thought you would soon come round to us after the letter. Sign that. You haven't been long. None of them are."

It was a receipt; and I was on the point of asking if it was to be signed in blood, when he settled the question by giving me the ink.

" There, Luke Lucraft, across the eight-penny stamp. I'm not allowed to answer any questions you may put, Mr. Lucraft, nor to ask you any; so take your money, and good-morning to you. I suppose, like the rest of them, you don't know the name of your benefactor, and would like to—yes ; but you needn't ask *me ;* and I've orders not to admit you to see either Mr. Charges or Mr. Crackett. They'd trouble enough with the last but one. He broke into their office once drunk, and laid about him with the ruler."

I burst into a cold dew of terror.

" However, Mr. Lucraft, I hope you will be more fortunate than your predecessors."

" Where are they ? Who are they ? "

" I do not know where they are, not for a certainty," he replied with a grin. " But we may guess. Dead and buried they are, all of them. Gone to kingdom come; all died of the same thing too—D.T. Delicious Trimmings killed them. Poor old gentleman! He's too good for this world, as everybody knows, and the more he's taken in the more he's deceived. Anyhow, he's very unlucky in his pensioners. He did say when the last went off that he would have no more; he wept over it, and declared that his bounty was always abused; but there never was such a benevolent old chap. I only wish he'd take a fancy to me."

"What did you say is his name, by the way?"

The clerk looked at me with a cunning wink.

"If you don't know, I am sure I do not," he said. "Here is the cheque, Mr. Lucraft, and I hope you will continue to come here and draw it a good deal longer than the other chaps. But there's a blight on all the pensioners.   Lord, what a healthy chap Tom Kirby—he was a Monmouth man—looked when he first came for his cheques!   As strong as a bull and as fresh as a lark."

"A good appetite had he?"

"No; couldn't eat anything after a bit; said he fancied nothing.   Lost his taste entirely.   He pined away and died in a galloping consumption before the third month was due.   Nobody ever saw him drinking, but he was drunk every night, regular, like the rest.   Perhaps it's only coincidence. Better luck to *you*, Mr. Lucraft!"

This conversation did not reassure me, and I determined to go over to Bucklersbury at once and see my patron.   I found the post against which I was leaning when he accosted me; there was no doubt about that, for the hares and the cauliflowers were still in the shop-windows, only they looked disgusting to me this morning.   I found the street into which he had led me, and then—then—it was the most extraordinary thing, I could not find the door by which we entered. Not only was there no door, but there seemed no place where such a door as I remembered could exist in this little winding narrow street. I went up and down twice. I looked at all the windows. I asked a policeman if he had ever seen an old gentleman about the street such as I described, or such a negro as Boule-de-neige; but he could give no information. Only as I prowled slowly along the pavement I heard distinctly—it gave me a nervous shock that I could not account for— the infernal " Cluck-cluck !" of the negro with the cold soft hands, the wrinkled skin, and the fiery red eyes. He was clucking at me from some hiding-place of his own, where he was safe. He had done me no harm that I knew of, but I hated him at that moment.

I was by this time not at all elated at my good fortune. I even craved to have back again what I had sold. I felt heavy at heart,

and had a presentiment of fresh trouble
before me. I thought of the fate of those
unknown and unfortunate predecessors, all
dead in consequence of drink, evil courses,
and D.T. Heavens! was I too to die
miserably with delirium tremens, after I had
sold my taste, and could only tell brandy
from water, like the cask which might hold
either, by the smell?

At half-past one—the luncheon time for
all who have appetites—the sense of being
gorged came upon me again, but this time
without the giddiness. I went to a tavern
in the Strand, and fell sound asleep. When
I awoke at six the oppression had passed
away. And now I began to realise something of the consequences of my act. I
say something, because worse, far worse,
remained behind. I was doomed, I saw
clearly, to be the victim of the old man's
gluttony. He would eat and I should suffer.
Already, as I guessed from the clerk's state-

ments, he had killed four strong men before
me. I was to be the fifth. I went again
to Bucklersbury, and sought in every house
for something that might give me a.clue. I
loitered in the quiet city streets in the hope
of finding my tormentor, and forcing him to
give me back my bond. There was no clue,
and I did not meet him. But I felt him. He
began dinner, as nearly as I could feel, about
seven o'clock; he took his meal with deliber-
ation, judging from the gradual nature of
my sensations; but he took an amazing
quantity, and by eight o'clock the weight
upon me was so great that I could scarcely
breathe. How I cursed my folly! How I
impotently writhed under the burden I had
wantonly laid upon myself! And then he
began to drink. The fiend, the scoundrel! I
felt the fumes mount to my head; there was
no exhilaration, no forgetfulness of misery;
none of the pleasant gradations of excitement,
hope, and confidence, through which men are

accustomed to pass before ariving at the final
stage, the complete oblivion, of intoxication.
I felt myself getting gradually but hopelessly
drunk.   I struggled against the feeling, but
in vain ; the houses went round and round
with me; my speech, when I tried to speak,
became thick ; the flags of the pavement flew
up and struck me violently on the forehead,
and I became unconscious of what happened
afterwards.

CHAPTER III.

In the morning I found myself lying on a stone bench in a small white-washed room. My brows were throbbing and my throat was parched, and in my brain was ringing, I do not know why, the infernal "Cluck-cluck!" of the negro with derisive iteration. I had not long to meditate; the door opened, and a constable appeared.

"Now then," he said roughly, "if you can stand upright by this time, come along."

It was clear enough to me now what had happened: I was in custody, in a police-cell, and I was going before a magistrate.

I dream of that ignominy still, though forty years have passed since I was placed in the dock and asked what I had to say for myself. "Drunk and disorderly."

I was charged by the constable—there were no police in 1823—with being drunk and disorderly. Twenty other poor wretches were waiting their trial for the same offence; one or two for graver charges. My case came first, and had the honour of being reported in the papers. Here is the extract cut out of the *Morning Chronicle*—

"A young man, who gave his name as Henry Luke, and said he was an actor by profession, was charged with being drunk and disorderly in the streets. The constable found him at ten o'clock lying on the pavement of Bucklersbury, too drunk even to speak, and quite unable therefore to give any account of himself. A cheque, signed by the well-known firm of Crackett & Charges, for £30 was found on his person. The magistrate remarked that this was a suspicious circumstance, and decided to remand the case till these gentlemen could be communicated with. One of the partners appeared at twelve, and deposed that the prisoner's real name was Luke Lucraft, that he had been an actor, and that the cheque had been given him by the firm, acting for a client who wished to be anonymous, but whose motive was pure benevolence.

" The magistrate, on hearing the facts of the case, addressed the prisoner with a suitable admonition. He bade him remember that such an abuse of a good man's charity, as he had been guilty of, was the worst form of ingratitude. It appeared, that on the very day of receiving a gift, which was evidently intended to advance him in life, or to find him the means of procuring suitable employment, the prisoner deliberately made himself so hopelessly drunk that he could neither speak nor stand—where, it did not appear. The magistrate could not but feel that this conduct showed the gravest want of moral principle,

and he strongly advised Mr. Crackett to
cancel the cheque till further orders. As,
however, it was a first offence, and in consideration of the prisoner's youth, the fine
inflicted would be a small one of ten shillings,
with costs."

That was the newspaper account of the
affair. On my way out of the court, Mr.
Crackett stopped me.

"Young man," he said, shaking his head,
"this is very dreadful. I warned my benevolent client against this act of generosity.
You are the fifth young man whom he has
assisted in this magnificent manner. The
former, all four, took to drink, and died in a
disgraceful manner. Take warning, and stop
while it is yet time."

I got away as fast as I could, and crept
back to my lodging after the necessary miserable breakfast.

I am not ashamed to say that I sat down
and cried. The tears *would* crowd into my

eyes. It was too dreadful. Here I was,
only twenty-four years of age, with my life
before me, doomed, through my own folly, to
a miserable ending and a disgraceful reputation. What good would come of having
money under these dreadful conditions ?
Money, indeed! What had become of the
fifty pounds given me only two days before ?
Gone. All gone but one single sovereign,
which served to pay my fine. Some one had
robbed me. Perhaps the constables. Perhaps
a street thief. It was gone. The sorry
reward of my consent to the unholy bargain
was clean swept away, and only the consequences of the contract remained.

In the afternoon, as I hastened home along
the darkening streets, hoping to reach my
lodging before the daily gorge began, a
curious thing happened to me. On the other
side of the street, in a dark corner, standing
upright, and pointing to me with a finger of
derision, I saw Boule-de-neige, the negro

servant. I rushed at him, blind with rage.
When I got to the spot I found nobody there.
Was it a trick of a disordered brain ? I had
seen him, quite plainly, grinning at me with
his wrinkled features. And as I turned from
the place I heard his familiar " Cluck-cluck."

Twice more on the way this strange phan-
tom appeared to me ; each time accompanied
by the " cluck " of his voice. · It was a phan-
tom with which I was to become familiar
indeed, before I had finished with Boule-de-
neige and his master.

It was clear that the demon to whom I had
sold myself was incapable of the slightest
consideration towards me. He would eat
and drink as much as he felt disposed to
do, careless of any consequences that might
befall me. It was equally evident that he
intended to make the most of his bargain, to
eat enormously every day, and to drink himself drunk every night. And I was powerless. Meantime it was becoming evident

that the consequences to me would be as serious as if I were myself guilty of these excesses. One drop of comfort alone remained: my appetite would fail, and my tormentor would be punished where he would feel it most. I lay down and waited till luncheon time; no sense of repletion came over me; it was certain, therefore, that he was already suffering a vicarious punishment, so to speak, for yesterday's debauch.

The next day, however, I really did meet my negro.

It was about five in the afternoon—the time when I was tolerably safe, because my owner, who took a plentiful luncheon at one, did not begin his nightly orgy much before seven. I was loitering about Bucklersbury, my favourite place of resort, in the hope of meeting the old man, when my arm was touched as I turned round. It *was* the negro. "Massa Lucraft," he said, "you come along o' me. Massa him berry glad to see you."

I declare that although the moment before I had been picturing such an encounter; although I had imagined myself with my fingers at his throat, dragging him off, and forcing him to tell me who and what he was, I felt myself unable to speak.

"Come along o' me, Massa Lucraft," he said; "this way—way you know berry well. Ho, ho!—Cluck."

He stopped before the door I remembered but had never been able to find, opened it with a little key, and led the way to the octagonal room.

There was no one in it, but the table was already laid for dinner.

"Massa come bymeby. You wait, young gegleman."

Then he disappeared somehow.

As before, I could see no door. As before, the first sensation which came over me was of giddiness, from which I recovered immediately. I walked round and round the room, looking at the heavy furniture, the pictures, which were all of fruit and game, and the silver plate. Everything showed the presence of great wealth, and, I supposed, though I knew nothing about it, great taste. I was kept waiting for nearly two hours. That I did not mind, because every moment brought me, I thought, nearer to the hour of my deliverance. I was certain that I had only to put the case to Mr. Grumbelow—I remembered his name the moment I was back in that room—to appeal to his generosity, his honour, his pity, in order to obtain my release. Mr. Grumbelow—Ebenezer Grumbelow—he was the charitable client of Messrs. Crackett & Charges, was he? Why, I might show him up to popular derision and hatred. I might tell the world who and what this great benefactor of young men really was.

Suddenly, as the clock struck seven, he stood upon the carpet before me, while Boule-de-neige stood at the table with a soup tureen in his hand. I declare that I did not see at any time any one enter the room or go out of it. They appeared to be suddenly in it.

I do hope that the appearance of small details like the above, at first incredible, will not be taken as proof of want of veracity on my own part. I wish that I could tell the tale without these particulars, but I cannot. I must relate the whole or none.

"You here?" said Mr. Grumbelow, looking at me with an air of contempt. He seated himself at the table and unfolded his napkin. "Soup, Boule-de-neige."

"Massa hungry? Dat young debbel there he look berry pale already."

"Pretty well, Boule-de-neige, considering. You, sir, come here, and let me look at you." I obeyed. "Hold out your hand. It shakes. Let me look at your eyes. They are yellow. Do you know that your appetite seems to me to be failing already—already—and it is only the fourth day."

" It is not my fault," I said.

" Nonsense. Don't talk to me, sir, because I will have none of your insolence. I say that you dó not walk enough. I order you to walk twelve miles a day—even twenty, after a heavy night—do you hear ? "

" It is not in the contract," I replied doggedly.

" It *is* in the contract. You are to use every means in your power to keep your faculties in vigour. What means have you used ? "

He banged the spoon on the table and glanced at me so fiercely that I had nothing to say.

" Massà, soup get cold," said Boule-de-neige.

He gobbled it up, every now and then looking up at me with an angry grunt.

" Now then, you and your contract. This is pretty ingratitude, this is. Here's a fellow, Boule-de-neige, I pick up out of the gutter, starving; whom I keep expensively; whom I endow with an income; whom I deprive of the temptation to gluttony."

"Nebber see such a debbel in all my days," said the negro; "nebber hear such a ting told nowhere."

"No, nor ever will. Listen to me, sir. You will walk ten, twelve, or twenty miles a day, according to the dinner I have had. And, mark you, it will be the worse for you if you do not. Remember, if I cannot eat I can drink."

There was a fiendish glare in his blood-stained eyes as he spoke, and I trembled. My spirit was so completely gone that I had not even the pluck to appeal to his pity. Perhaps a secret consciousness of the use-lessness of such an appeal deterred me.

"You will now," he said, "watch me making as large a dinner as your miserably languid appetite will allow."

"I have been drunk for four nights," I pleaded.

" Then you have no business to get drunk so easily. Your head is contemptibly weak—what did I take yesterday, Boule-de-neige?"

" Big bottle champagne, big bottle port, eight goes whisky grog."

" I did—and that was all. Why your predecessor stood double the quantity."

" Beg pardon, massa. Last young gegleman poor trash—last but two—him mighty strong head — head like bull — nebber get drunk."

" Ah, we wasted him, Boule-de-neige; we fooled him away in one imprudent evening. I told you at the time that ncyeau punch is a very dangerous thing."

" Ho, ho!" the diabolical negro laughed till his teeth showed like the grinning jaws of a death's head. " Ho, ho! him so blind drunk he tumble out of window—break him neck. Ho, ho!"

This was a pleasant conversation for me to hear.

Then Mr. Grumbelow resumed his dinner.

He ate a good deal in spite of his grumbling, and then he began to drink port. I observed that the wine had a peculiar effect upon him. It made him redder in the face, but not thicker in speech. He drank two bottles, talking at me all the time. I began to get drunk, he only got the more merrily fiendish.

"This is really delightful," he said, as I reeled and caught at a chair for support. "I wonder I never thought of this before. It is quite a new pleasure to watch the effects of my own drink on another man's brain. I shall write a book about you. I shall call it 'The Young Christian deterred, or Leaves from Luke Lucraft's Wicked Life.' Ho, ha! ha, ho! I saw the account in the *Morning Post*. Heigh, heigh!"—he nearly choked as he recalled the circumstance. "The magistrate admonishing the wicked drunkard. Ho, ho! It is like a farce. Stand up, sir,

stand up. He can't stand up. Can you
sing? Can you dance? He could not even
dance a hornpipe. Do you feel a little
thickness in your speech? Would you be
able to explain to the worthy magistrate the
circumstances quite beyond your own control,
which brought you into that painful position
in which you stood? It is the best situation
that ever was put upon any stage. There's
nothing like it in fiction. Nothing. Walter
Scott never invented anything half so rich.
Ho, ho, ho! he is really getting drunk
already. What a poor creature it is!"

He paused for a moment and then went
on.

" Boule-de-neige, coffee; brandy in it—
plenty of brandy, and a glass of curaçoa afterwards. A large glass, sir! I'll have a night
of it. Your health, Luke Lucraft, in this
coffee; and you had better take care of it, or
I'll pack you off with noyeau punch. Pleasant times you are having, eh? Might have

been worse, you know. You might have been
starving—What? Don't fall against the table
in that way. Take care of the furniture.
It cost a great deal more money than you
are worth. So, sit down on the floor while
I tell you about your predecessors, dead and
gone, poor fellows.

"Let me see. The first was William
Saunders, a poor devil of a clerk of mine.
He disgraced himself in chapel one week-
day prayer-meeting, the very evening of
his signature; then he ran away, but Boule-
de-neige found him out, and brought him
back. He took to praying and crying.
One day he died in Bartholomew Hospital
of delirium tremens. He lasted about six
months.

"The next was Hans Hansen, a Dane.
He only lasted about three weeks, because
he became melancholy directly he found he
could no longer taste brandy. I was disappointed with Hansen, and when he jumped

off London Bridge into the Thames one night, his appetite having quite gone, I was really very sorry on account of the temporary inconvenience it put me to; and I determined to be very careful in his successor. I remember I had a good deal of trouble to find one.

"However, at last I got a third man, a stout Cumberland chap, son of a statesman. You poor, puny, little strolling actor, I suppose that you will hardly believe that I once took four and twenty tumblers of Scotch whisky and water without affecting that brave fellow's appetite one bit. He used to take it out in swearing; and really he was almost too often in trouble with the magistrates. He never clearly understood that his safety lay in being home early in the evening. Once he nearly killed Mr. Crackett in his own office. Poor Crackett! that eminent Christian lawyer; I should never have forgiven myself had anything happened to the worthy Crackett.

Well! he went too; at least, after a good tough twelvemonth. It was my own fault, and I ought not to grumble. That noyeau punch was strong enough to kill the devil."

"Cluck," said Boule-de-neige.

"Then we came to Tom Kirby. None of them looked so well or promised so much; none broke down so easily. A whining · fellow too; a crying, sobbing, appealing rogue, who wanted to get off his bargain. However, de mortuis—— Your health, Luke Lucraft. Hallo! hold up."

"I tell you what I mean to do after you are worked off, Luke Lucraft. I mean to have a brace of fellows. I shall go down to the London docks or else to the railway stations, and find a couple of trusty young porters. They are the sort of men to have. Fine, strong, well-set-up rascals. Men with muscles like rigging ropes—don't clutch at the chairs, Lucraft—if you can't sit up you may lie down—I shall make them come here

—give them a blow out of steak—I wasted a splendid dinner on you—and then I shall make them sign.

" The great thing, then, will be to have the appetites of two men; twice as much to eat and twice as much to drink. I never thought of that before.

"And then to bring both the rogues up here of an evening and make them wait and see me eat; watch them gradually lolling and reeling about till they tumble over each other; go secretly and hear them curse me, me their benefactor—Ho! ho! I think I shall not be long over you, Luke Lucraft, Hallo! keep your drunken legs away from the table. Boule-de-neige, roll this intoxicated log into the street."

CHAPTER IV.

WHEN I came to my senses it was of course
the next morning, and I was lying in my own
bed-room, whither I had been carried by two
strange men, the landlady afterwards told
me, who said they were paid for the job.
I had a splitting headache. I was sick and
giddy; my limbs trembled beneath me when
I tried to stand; my hands shook. I looked
at myself in the glass. Swollen features and
bloodshot eyes greeted me.

Less than a week had wrought this ruin.

The ordinary drunkard refreshes himself in
the morning with tea. Nothing refreshed me
because I could taste nothing, and because
my suffering sprang from a different source,

though they were the same in kind. I had
to bear them as best I might.

I remembered the command which Mr.—
Mr.—strange, I had forgotten his name
again—gave me, to walk twenty miles after a
" heavy night." I started to obey him.

Outside London, beyond Islington, where
there are now rows of houses, but were then
fields, I saw a little modest cottage, standing
alone in its garden. It was a cottage with
four rooms only, covered over with creepers.
On a board, standing at the gate, was
an announcement that it was to let. A
thought struck me. Here could be seclusion,
at any rate. Here I could shut myself up
every night, and await in comparative safety
the dreadful punishment — fast becoming
heavier than I could bear — which my
tormentor inflicted upon me. Why should
I not take the cottage, pay the rent in
advance every month—for how many months
should I have to pay it ?—and so wait in

patience and resignation the approach of my inevitable fate ?

I made inquiries at once, and secured the place at a merely nominal rent. Then I moved in a little furniture, bought second-hand in Islington High Street, and became the occupant, a lonely hermit, of the house. There were no houses within hearing in case I should storm and rage in my drunken madness at night. The cottage stood removed from the road, and no callers were likely to trouble me. Within those walls I should be secure from some dangers at least. Here, night after night, I could await the attacks of surfeit and intoxication, which regularly came ; for my master knew no pity.

On the first evening I sat down at half-past six to prepare for what was coming. The day was drawing in, and a cold twilight—the month was March—covered the trees and shrubs in my little garden, as I opened the door and looked out.

Before me stood the negro.

My spirit was quite broken, and I could only groan.

" Do you want me to go with you again ? " I asked, thinking of the last entertainment at which I provided amusement for his master.

" Massa say him berry glad you come hyar. You walk the twenty mile ebbery day, else massa know the reason why. How you feel, Massa Lucraft ? Heigh ! heigh ! cluck. Dat most fortunate day for you when you sign dat little paper."

He delivered his message and disappeared in the darkness. I heard his footsteps crunching the gravel in the road, and I longed, only now I had no courage or spirit left, to seize him and tear him limb from limb.

Then I shut myself in, lit one candle, and sat over the fire. I thought of the scenes by which my extravagant fancy had been excited; the garden full of lively girls—what were girls to me now ? the country walks I

was to have with Juliet—where was my
passion for Juliet now? The ease and happiness, the lightness and innocence, of the life
before me, drawn by that arch-deceiver, compared with my present, my actual misery,
sitting alone, cut off from mankind, the slave
and victim of a secret·profligate and glutton,
doomed to die slowly, unless it should please
the murderer to kill me off quickly.

And then, because the first symptoms of
the attack were coming on, I went to bed and
stayed there.

So began my new life. A wretched life it
was. There was no occupation possible for
me—no amusement. I walked every day, in
fair weather or foul, a measured twenty miles.

This in some degree restored vitality to
my system. I never read. I took no interest
in any politics. I sat by myself, and brooded.

As for my meals, I bought them ready
prepared. They consisted almost wholly of
bread and cold mutton. You may judge of

the absolutely tasteless condition to which I
was reduced, when I write calmly and truthfully that cold boiled mutton was as agreeable
to me as any other form of food.   I found,
after repeated trials, that mutton forms the
best fuel—it is better than either beef or
pork—and keeps the human engine at work
for the longest time. So I had mutton. As I
discovered also that bulk was necessary, and
that only a certain amount of animal food
was wanted, I used to have cold potatoes
always ready. I stoked twice a day, at eleven
in the morning and about five in the afternoon.   Thus fortified, I got through the
miserable hours as best as I could.

I look back on that period as one of
unmitigated misery and despair.   I was daily
growing more bloated, fatter, and flabbier in
the cheeks.   My hands trembled in the
morning.   I seemed losing the power of
connected thought.   My very lips were
thickening.

I hope I am making it clear what was the
effect of my bargain on myself—I mean without reference to the sufferings inflicted on me
by my tyrant. People, however, never can
know, unless they happen to be like myself,
which is unlikely, how great a part eating and
drinking take in the conduct of life. Between
the rest of the world and me there was a
great gulf fixed. They could enjoy, I could
not ; they could celebrate every joyful event
with something additional to eat ; they could
make a little festival of every day ; they
could give to happiness an outward and
tangible form. Alas, not only was I debarred
from this, but I was cut off even from joy
itself! for, if you look at it steadily, you will
find that most of human joy or suffering is
connected with the senses. I had bartered
away a good half of mine, and the rest
seemed in mourning for the loss of their
fellows. As for my pale and colourless life,
it was as monotonous as the clock. If I

neglected to stoke, the usual feebleness would follow.   There was no gracious looking forward to a pleasant dinner; no trembling anticipations in hope and fear of what might be preparing; no cheerful contemplation of the joint while the carver sharpens his knife; no discussions of flavour and richness; no modestly hazarded conclusions as to more currants; no rolling of the wine-glass in the fingers to the light and smacking of lips over the first sip—all these things were lost to me. Reader, if haply this memoir ever see a posthumous light, think what would happen to yourself if eating and drinking, those perennial joys of humanity, which last from the infantine pap to the senile Revalenta Arabica, were taken away.

All things tasted alike, as I have said, and cold mutton formed my staple dish.   As I could only distinguish between beer, wine, coffee, and tea by the look, I drank water. If I ventured, which was seldom, to take my

dinner at a cookshop, I would choose my
pièce de résistance by the look, by some fancied
grace in the shape, but not by taste or smell.
The brown of roast beef might attract me
one day and repel me the next. I was
pleased with the comeliness of a game-pie,
or tickled by some inexplicable external
charm of a beefsteak-pudding. But three
quarters of my life were gone, and with them
all my happiness.

If you have no appetite for eating, you can
enjoy nothing in the whole world. That is
an axiom. I could not taste, therefore my
eye ceased to feel delight in pleasant sights,
and my ear in pleasant sounds. It was not
with me as in the case of a blind man, that
an abnormal development of some other
sense ensued; quite the contrary. In selling
one, I seem to have sold them all. For,
as I discovered, man is one and inseparable;
you cannot split him up; and when my arch-
deceiver bought my appetite, he bought me

out and out. A wine-merchant might as well pretend to sell the bouquet of claret and preserve the body ; or a painter the colour of his picture and preserve the drawing ; or a sculptor the grace of his group and keep the marble.

As regards other losses, I found I had lost the perception of beauty in form or colour. Why this was so I cannot explain. I was no longer, I suppose, in harmony with other men on any single point. Pretty women passed me unheeded ; pictures had no charm for me ; music was only irritating to my nerves.

Then I found that I had lost the power of sympathy. I had formerly been a soft-hearted man. I remarked now that the sight of suffering found me entirely callous. There was a poor family living about half a mile from me, whose acquaintance I made through buying some of my supplies of them. They were in distress for rent ; they applied to

me . . . . there, I cannot bear to think of
it. I had the money and I refused them.
They were sold up, and I sat at my door and
watched them on their way to London—the
mother, the two girls, the little boy, hand-
in-hand, homeless and penniless, without a
pang and without a single prompting of the
heart to help them. God knows what became
of them. May He forgive me for the hard-
hearted cruelty with which I regarded their
fate.

Had I, then, sold everything to this man?

I had been pretty religious in a way—a
young man's way. Now I had lost all religious feeling whatever. I had once ambition
and hopes, these were gone; I had once the
capacity of love, that was gone; I had once
a generous heart, that was gone; I once
loved things worth loving, I felt no emotion
now for anything. I was a machine which
could feel. I was a man with the humanity
taken out of him.

This time lasted for about four months. On the first of each month I went to receive my pay—the wages of sin—from the clerk, who surveyed me critically, but said nothing till the morning of the fourth month. Then, while he handed me my money, he whispered confidentially across the table :

" Look here, old fellow, you know ; you're going it, worse than poor Tom Kirby. Why don't you stop it ? What *is* the good of a feller's drinking himself to death ? The old gentleman was here yesterday, asking me how you looked and if you continued steady. Pull up, old man, and knock it off."

I took the money in my trembling hands and slunk away abashed. When I got home again, I am not ashamed to say that I cried like a child.

Delirium tremens ! That would begin soon, and then the end would not be far off. It was too awful. Think of my position. I was but four and twenty. Not only was I deprived of the pleasure—mind you, a very real pleasure—of eating and drinking ; I was the most temperate man in the world, though that was no great credit to myself, considering ; and yet I bore in my face and my appearance, and felt in my very brain, all the marks and signs of confirmed drunkenness and the hopelessness of it. That hardened old voluptuary, that demon of gluttony, that secret murderer, would have no pity. He must have felt by the falling-off of the splendid appetite which he was doing his utmost to ruin, that things were getting worse, and he was resolved—I had suspected this for some time—to kill me off by drinking me to death.

I believe I should have been dead in another week, but for a blessed respite, due, I afterwards discovered, to my demon being laid up with so violent a sore throat that he could not even swallow. What was my joy at being able to go to bed sober, to

wake without a headache, to feel my bad
symptoms slowly disappearing, to recover
my nerves! For a whole fortnight I was
happy—so happy that I even believed the
improvement would last and that the old
man was penitent. One day, after fourteen
days of a veritable earthly paradise, I was
walking along the Strand — for I was no
longer afraid of venturing out—and met my
old manager, Juliet's father. He greeted
me with a warmth that was quite touching
under all the circumstances. "My dear boy,
I have been longing to know your where-
abouts. Come and tell me all about it.
Have you dined? Let us have some dinner
together."

I excused myself, and asked after Juliet.

"Juliet is but so-so. Ah, do you know,
Lucraft, sometimes I think that I did wrong
to part you. And yet, you know, you had
no money. Make some, my boy, and come
back to us."

This was hearty. I forgot my troubles and my state of bondage and everything, except Juliet.

"I—I—I have money," I said. "I have come into a little money unexpectedly."

"Have you?" he replied, clasping me by the hand. "Then come down and see Juliet. Or—stay; no. The day after to-morrow is Juliet's ben. We are playing at Richmond. We have one of your own parts—you shall be Sir Harry Wildair. I will alter the bills. You are sure to come?"

"Sure to come," I said with animation. "Capital! I know every line in the part. Tell Juliet that an old friend will act with her."

We made a few new arrangements and parted. I bought a copy of the play at Lacy's, and studied the part over again.

Next day I got over to Richmond in good time. The day was fine, I remember; my spirits were rapidly rising because it was now the fifteenth day since I had had one of my usual attacks. I was in great hopes that the old man was really going to change his life and behave with consideration towards me. With the birth of hope, there revived in my heart some of my old feelings. I had a real desire to see Juliet again, but yet the old warmth seemed gone. It was a desire to see one in whom I had once been interested; the desire to awake old memories which, I think, principally actuated me.

I found the dear girl waiting for me with an impatience which ought to have touched my heart, but which, somehow, only seemed to remind me of old times. My heart was gone — sold to my master with everything else. Mechanically I took her hands in mine, and kissed her on the lips as I used to do. She threw both arms round my neck, kissed me again and again, and burst into tears of joy.

"Oh, Luke, Luke!" she said, "I have so longed to see you again. The time has been weary, weary, without you."

We sat together for half an hour, she all the time talking to me, and I, remembering what I used to be with her, wondering where the old feelings were gone, and trying to act as I used to.

"Luke, you are not growing cold to me, are you?" she asked, as some little gesture or word of hers passed me unnoticed.

"Cold, Juliet?" I replied. "What should make you think so?"

"I will not think so," she said. "It is too great happiness to meet again, is it not? And you are silent because you feel too happy to speak. Is not that so?"

Presently it became time to go and dress.

"Let me look at you, Sir Henry Wildair," she said. "Yes, we shall do it very well to-night. You are not looking, somehow, quite so well as you used, Luke dear. Is it that

London does not agree with you? Are you working too hard? Your face is swollen and —fancy—Mrs. Mould says you look as if you had been drinking."

Mrs. Mould was the dresser.

If Mrs. Mould had seen me a fortnight before, she might well have said I had been drinking. A fortnight, however, of rest had done wonders for me.

I laughed, but felt a little uneasy.

We rang up at seven.

The house was quite full, because my Juliet was popular at Richmond.

I began with all my former fire and vigour, because I was acting again with her. The old life came back to me; I forgot my troubles; I was really happy, and I believe I acted well. At all events, the house applauded. Between the first and second act a sudden terror seized me. I felt that the old man was eating again. That passed off, because he ate very little. But then he began to drink, and to drink fast.

It was no use fighting against it. I believe the villain must have been drinking raw brandy, because I was drunk in five minutes. I staggered and reeled about on the stage, I laughed wildly and sang foolishly, and then I tumbled down in a heap and could not get up again. The last thing I remember is the angry roar of poor old Kerrans, beside himself with passion, telling the carpenters to carry that drunken beast away and throw him into the road. I heard afterwards that they were obliged to drop the curtain, and that the *éclat* of poor Juliet's benefit was entirely spoiled. As for myself, the carpenters carried me out to the middle of Richmond-green, where they were going to leave me, only one of them had compassion, and wheeled me to his own house in a barrow.

In the morning I returned hastily to London, sought my cottage at Islington, and shut myself in with an agony of shame and humiliation.

I was quite crushed by this blow. For the first time I felt tempted to commit suicide and end it all. To be sure I ought to have foreseen this, and all the other dreadful things. Directly my master, my owner, got able to swallow, though he could not eat, he could drink, and ordered the most fiery liquor he could procure, with a view to kill me off and begin with another victim.

But Providence ruled otherwise.

Then began a week of cruel suffering. My master sent me word by Boule-de-neige that he intended to finish me off. My appetite, he said, had been long failing, and was now perfectly contemptible. He complained that I had neglected my part of the contract, that I must have been practising intemperance—the horrible hypocrite—to have reduced so fine an appetite to nothing in a short four months. Therefore he felt obliged to tell me that in a week or two I should probably find the agreement ended. That was his ferocious

way of putting it. He meant that in a week
I should be dead. His words were prophetic,
but not in the sense in which he meant them.

He drank brandy now. He drank it morning, noon, and night. He drank it, not
because he liked it, but in hopes of despatch-
ing me. I was no sooner partially recovered
from one drunken bout than I plunged into
another.

I lost all power of walking. I could not
move about. I lay the whole day sick and
feverish on my bed, or, if I got up at all, it
was only to change it for an easy chair. I
could eat nothing.

Then I· began to have visions and to see
spectres in my loneliness and misery.

First I saw all over again the scenes of my
early life—my poor deserted mother; the
tramp who took charge of me; the sleep in
which I nearly perished; the strolling actors
with whom I wandered; the girl with whom
I fell in love. Only among them all there

hovered perpetually the ugly face of Boule-
de-neige, spoiling the pleasant memories,
and corrupting the current of my thoughts
with his " cluck, cluck," and his demoniac
grin.

" How you do, Massa Lucraft ?   How you
feel your stumjack this morning ?   Ole massa
him berry fierce.   Him gwine to make the
noyeau punch to-morrow.   Dat finish um
off.   Dat work um up.   You wait till to-
morrow, Massa Lucraft."

I could only groan.

" You nice young gegleman," he went on
with a grin.   " You berry grateful young·
gegleman.   Massa him gib you thirty pounds
a month, and you spend it all in 'temperate
courses.   Bad ; berry bad ; dam bad.   What
you say when you die—eh ?   Ho ! ho !"

The creature seemed always with me
during this time.   If I opened my eyes I
had the feeling that he was hovering about
my bed.   If it was dark I thought I saw his

eyes glaring at me from some corner. If I
was asleep he would waken me with his
"cluck." What he did in my cottage I never
knew. The room was filled with the visions
which passed through my brain, succeeding
each other again and again like the acts of
a play repeated incessantly. I saw the
octagonal room with the old gentleman eating and drinking. I saw myself at Richmond. I saw myself before the magistrates ;
and I looked on as an outsider, as a spectator
of a tragedy which would end in death and
horror.

It was two days before the period allotted
to me by my master, at eight o'clock in the
evening, as I was sitting in my lonely cottage,
expectant of the usual drunken bout, when I
felt a curious agitation within me, an internal
struggle, as if through all my veins a tem-
pestuous wave was surging and rushing. I
lay down.

"This is some new devilry of the old

man," I said to myself. "Let him do his worst; at least, I must try to bear it with resignation." I began to speculate on my inevitable and approaching end, and to wonder curiously what proportion of the sin of all this drunkenness would be laid to my charge.

To my astonishment nothing more followed. The tumult of my system gradually subsided, and I fell asleep.

In the morning I awoke late, and missed the usual headache. I had therefore, I was surprised to find, actually not been drunk the night before. I rose with my customary depression, and was astonished to discover that my nerves were steadier and spirits higher than I had known for a long time.

I mechanically went to the cupboard and pulled out my cold mutton and potatoes. Who can picture my joy when I found that I could taste the meat again, and that it was nasty? I hardly believed my senses; in fact, I had lost them for so long, that it was difficult to understand that they had come back to me. I tried the potatoes. Heavens, what a horrible thing to a well-regulated palate is a cold boiled potato !

At first, as I said, I could not believe that I had recovered my taste ; then, as the truth forced itself upon me, and I found that I could not only taste, but was actually hungry, I jumped and danced, and was beside myself with joy. Think of a convict suddenly re-leased, and declared guiltless of the charges brought against him. Think of a prisoner on the very ladder of the gallows-tree, with the rope round his neck, reprieved and pardoned. Think of one doomed to death by his physician receiving the assurance that it was all a mistake, and that he would gather up long years of life as in a sheaf. And think that such joy as these would feel, I felt —and more !

I went to the nearest coffee-shop and

ordered bacon, eggs, and tea, offering up a short grace with every plate as it came. And, then, because I felt sure that my old tormentor must be dead, I repaired to my lawyers, and saw the clerk.

" Ah," he said, " the poor old man's gone at last! Went out like the snuff of a candle. His illness was only twenty-four hours. Well, he's gone to heaven if ever man did."

"What did he die of—too much eating and drinking ?"

" Mr. Lucraft," said the clerk severely, " this is not the tone for *you* to adopt towards that distinguished man, your benefactor. He died, sir—being a man of moral, temperate, and even abstemious life, though of full habit —of apoplexy."

" O !" I said, careless what the clerk said, but glad to be quite sure that the diabolical old villain was really dead. I suppose that never was such joy over the repentance of any sinner as mine over the death of that murdering glutton, for whom no words of hatred were too strong.

" I think you've got to see our senior partner," said the clerk.   " Step this way."

He led me to a room where I found a grave and elderly gentleman sitting at a table.

" Mr. Lucraft ? " he said.   " I was expecting you.   I saw your late patron's negro this morning.   He told me that you would call."

I stared, but said nothing.

" I have a communication to make to you, on the part of our departed friend, Mr. Ebenezer Grumbelow.   It is dated a few weeks since, and is to the effect that a sum of money which I hold was to be placed in your hands in case of his death.   This, it appears, he anticipated, for some reason or other."

" Ebenezer Grumbelow."   That was the name which had so long escaped my memory —" Ebenezer Grumbelow."

I said nothing, but stared with all my eyes.

"My poor friend," the lawyer went on, "after remarking that unless you change your unfortunate habits you will come to no good, gave me this money himself—here is the cheque—so that it will not appear in his last will and testament."

I took it in silence.

"Well, sir"—he looked at me in some surprise—"have you no observation to make, or remark to offer, on this generosity?"

"None," I said.

"I do not know," he continued; "I do not know—your signature here, if you please—what reason Mr. Grumbelow had in taking you up, or what claim you possessed upon his consideration: but I think, sir, I do think, that some expression, some sense of regret, is due."

I buttoned up the check in my pocket.

"Mr. Grumbelow was a philanthropist, I believe, sir?"

" He was.   As a philanthropist, as a supporter of charities, as a public donor of great amounts, Mr. Grumbelow's name stands in the front.   So much we all know."

" A religious man, too ? "

" Surely, surely ; one of our most deeply religious men.   A man who was not ashamed of his saintly profession."

" Cluck-cluck ! "

It was the familiar face of Boule-de-neige at the door.

" You know, I suppose," said the lawyer, " Mr. Grumbelow's body-servant, a truly Christian negro ? "

" Was there," I asked, " any clause in Mr. Grumbelow's letter—any conditions attached to this gift ? "

" None whatever.   It is a free gift.   Stay, there is a postscript which I ought to have read to you.   You will perhaps understand it. In it Mr. Grumbelow says that as to the services rendered by him to you, and by you to him, it will be best for your own sake to keep them secret."

I bowed.

The date of the cheque corresponded with the first illness of the old man—his affection of the throat. Probably he was afraid that I should reveal his infamous story.

" I may now tell you, Mr. Lucraft, without at all wishing to break any confidence that may have existed between you and the deceased, that a friend of Mr. Grumbelow's—no other, indeed, than the Rev. Jabez Jumbles, a pulpit name doubtless known to you—intends to write the biography of this distinguished and religious man, as an example to the young.. Any help you can afford to so desirable an end will be gratefully received. Particularly, Mr. Lucraft, any communication on the subject of his continual help given to young men, who regularly disappointed him, and all, except yourself, died of drink."

I bowed again and retired.

Did any one ever hear of such a wicked old man?

Outside the office I was joined · by the negro.

"What have you got to say to me, detestable wretch?" I cried, shaking my fist in his withered old face.

"Cluck-cluck! Massa not angry with poor old Boule-de-neige. How young massa? Young massa . pretty well? How de lubly abbadide of de young gegleman? How him strong stumjack? Cluck-cluck!"

He kept at a safe distance from me. I think I should have killed him if I had ever clutched him by the throat.

·"Ole massa him always ask, 'How dat young debbel? Go and see, Boule-de-neige.' I go to young massa's cottage daraway, and come back, 'Him berry dam bad, sir,' I say; 'him going to de debbel berry fast, just like dem oders. De folk all say he drink too much for him berry fine con-

stitution.' Cluck-cluck! Ole massa he only
say say ebbery night, 'Bring de brandy,
Boule-de-neige; let's finish him.' Cluck-
cluck!"

Here was a Christian negro for you!

"Tell me, what did your master die
of?"

"Apple perplexity, massa."

"Ah; what else? Come, Boule-de-neige,
I know a good deal; tell me more."

"Massa's time up," he whispered, coming
close to me. "Time quite up, and him berry
much 'fraid. Massa Lucraft want servant?
Boule-de-neige berry good servant. Cook
lubly dinner; make massa rich, like Massa
Grumbelow."

"I'd rather hire the devil!" I exclaimed.

"Cluck-cluck-cluck!" grinned the creature;
and really he looked at the moment as much
like the devil as one could wish. "Cluck!
dat massa can do if massa like."

I rushed away, too much excited by the

recovery of my freedom to regard what he said.

I was free ! What next ?

First, the restoration of my shattered nerves.

There was no permanent injury done to my constitution, because, after all, the drink had not actually gone down my throat, nor was it I who had consumed the gallons of turtle-soup, the tons of fish, the shiploads of cattle with which he had punished me for that woful signature of mine.

The contract, in some inexplicable manner, affected me with the punishment of my purchaser's excesses by a kind of sympathy. I remained a strictly temperate man for a month. I recovered gradually the tone of my system ; my features lost their bloated look. I became myself again.

And then I sought the injured Kerrans.

It was no use trying to tell him a story which he never would have believed. I

simply told him that I was taken suddenly
and hopelessly ill on that fatal night. I asked
him to remember, which is quite true, how I
began the piece with a fire and animation
quite impossible in a man who had been
drinking ; how I had certainly nothing between the scenes, during which intervals I
was talking with him, and how the thing
came upon me without any warning. If you
try, you know, you can make yourself quite
drunk with brandy in two minutes. This is
just what Mr. Grumbelow did to me.

Kerrans, good fellow, outraged in his
best feelings, was difficult to smooth down.

He had asked me to act with Juliet in the
hope of restoring to the girl her lost good
spirits. I came ; the misfortune happened,
and she was worse than ever. But he for-
gave me at last, and allowed me another
chance. This time it was not Juliet who
threw her arms around me, it was I who
implored her forgiveness, and the renewal of

her love. I was cold no longer. I left off remembering, and lived again in the present. I was a lover, and my girl was trembling and blushing, with her hand in mine.

It all happened more than fifty years ago. The only records which remain of the events I have described are on the tablet to the memory of Ebenezer Grumbelow in St. Rhadegunda's Church, City; and the little faded scrap from the *Morning Chronicle*, which I always carry in my pocket-book, and which tells the tale of my shame.

Juliet never believed my story, and I left off insisting on its truth.

She lies in Norwood Cemetery now, but we kept our golden wedding ere she died; and children and grandchildren live to bless her name.

MYSTERY OF JOE MORGAN.

If everybody would take the trouble, once for all, to set down his own personal experiences, and no other's, among the world of spirits, we might be spared a good deal of controversy, and those unfortunates, now in the minority, who, having nothing to commu‑ nicate, do the scoffing, would see the necessity of changing their note. I am in daily expectation of seeing this modification of the enemy's front : I look for the day when they will sing, like Scarron, " Désormais il faut filer doux." But in all ages men have scoffed at the world of spirits—until their first ghost.

To those who know and understand, it is
curious to mark the sudden change from
scepticism—even open infidelity—to the reverent awe produced by a single Appearance.
I know by my own experience that the tran-
sition is at first almost too great to be borne,
like the sudden passage from darkness into
dazzling light.   It is not, however, my intention to defend or to attack the credibility of
the supernatural : I have only to set down in
plain terms, and for what it is worth, my own
single experience among the residents of the
other world.

One difficulty I may be allowed to mention.
Since so few ghosts are ever seen or heard of,
what becomes of all the rest ?   There are, at
present, about 900,000,000 men, women, and
children breathing these upper airs.   Every
30 years a third of these have disappeared
and been replaced.   Supposing the process
to have been going on for 3,000 years, which
is not an undue estimate, considering the

vestiges of ancient civilisation and a teeming population which surround us on all sides, we get for the number of souls which have been born into the world during that period the total of 900,000,000,000—an army which, allowing $2\frac{1}{2}$ square feet for every one, would occupy 81,000 square miles for mere standing room, or a territory not quite 300 miles square. Of all these 900,000,000,000 how few there are who ever condescend to show themselves to living man! and yet how small a space they occupy all together! It seems to me, speaking as one having but little knowledge of the other world, that the few visits we receive from our ancestors argues a studied slight put upon living men by the majority. After all, the living, and not the dead, are the representatives of humanity.

I was engaged, five years ago, to the young lady whom I have since married. The engagement had little romance about it. We.

met, we saw, we conquered each other.
Eleanor's parents made fewer objections than
I feared, my fears being based upon the usual
grounds. I was given to understand that the
duration of the engagement depended entirely
upon myself, and, as I was already perilously
near thirty, I hastened to bring matters to
a speedy termination. The remarkable hin-
drance to the realisation of my hopes, arising
out of circumstances entirely unlooked for
and beyond my control, forms the subject of
this paper. It was not a pleasant experience:
and yet it gives me a sense of pleasure to
recall it ; just as an old salt will delight in
dwelling on the dangers of the ocean. There
is nothing, strictly speaking, horrible about it.
At the same time, when I write it down in
cold blood, I am conscious of a tingling of the
nerves and a tendency to look over the left
shoulder. This, I suppose, will never leave
me. It is a distinction, I know—perhaps a
small one, like the Companionship of the

Bath, or that of the order of St. Michael
and St. George, or the queer Turkish decor-
ations with which old Crimean officers love
to decorate themselves—but still a distinction.
It is not everybody, even now, who can tell
of visits from the other world ; and the constant companionship of a ghost seems to me
—naturally inclined to exaggerate on such a
subject—an adventure, perhaps, a little out of
the common.

I had taken and furnished, in readiness for
my wedding, a small detached villa, some
few miles out of London ; it was a new
house, with—though I did not think of that
— no possible memories of the past to
awaken disagreeable thoughts : a pretty little
house, standing between a lawn on the front
and a garden behind ; with stables on one
side and a " library " built out on the other.
There were the usual trees in the front—a
laburnum, a lilac, a laurestinus, a row of
limes, enough to shade the house from the

road and give the appearance of privacy
such as every Londoner loves. But it was
not a gloomy house. It stood east and
west, so that the drawing-room, which ran
the whole depth of the house, was never
without sunshine whenever there might be
any going. The view from the back was
perfectly cheerful; beyond the garden lay
green fields, and beyond these stretched a
noble park studded with elms: a bright,
cheerful, and comfortable house. On the
north, separated by several houses, and out
of sight, therefore out of mind, was a cemetery, belonging to a great town parish, newly
laid out and, as yet, thinly populated. Had
I noticed it at all, I should have laughed
at the idea of spectres in connection with
so smiling a garden. Ghosts, I might have
said, prowl about grim old churchyards whose
falling tombstones are green with moss, on
whose slabs clings the yellow lichen, where
the grass grows tall and rank, and the

brambles stretch long, thorny arms across
the paths, whose worn stones once preserved
the names of the long-forgotten dead. They
love the old country God's-acre, piled eight
and ten feet high with human mould, where
every pinch of dust contains what is left of
a life once filled with hopes and fears. But
not a new cemetery: not a formal place
planted with roses, laid out in gravel walks,
and lying round two perky little chapels
which stand face to face, turning up spiteful
noses at each other, and breathing a post-
mortem defiance. Is there a Bogey-ridden
boy living who would fear to pass a night
in Finchley Cemetery, or dread to sit out a
few dark hours alone in Nunhead?

I was mistaken. The truth is that the new-
ness of a cemetery is no proof of its tran-
quillity. Comparatively rare as are the visits
of ghosts, they may come from a cemetery
handselled only a week ago, a mere upstart
thing of yesterday, as well as from a grave-

yard whose long annals are dark with the
secrets of a thousand unknown murders.
One is never safe, and the only way to insure
immunity from these generally unwelcome
visitors is, perhaps, to live as far as possible
from a churchyard of any kind. I have
been particular in describing my house, because I wish it clearly understood that there
was not, either about the place or its neighbourhood, any predisposition to ghosts. Nor
was there about myself. I am not an imaginative man : there are no poems, romances,
or novels with my name to them. I have
no patience with people who can forget their
own real troubles in reading of those which
never happened; and, for the life of me, I
cannot have any interest in the loves of
anybody but myself. I am not, therefore,
a man likely to be the prey of hallucinations.
I am no puling poet trembling at a shadow,
nor am I one of those poor spectre-smitten
imbeciles who turn a branch into a warn-

ing finger, and a snow-drift into a sheeted wraith. This consideration makes my trifling experience the more credible.

The situation is this. An unimaginative man of thirty, whose days are spent in business; a new suburban villa; a bright, sunshiny country; neighbours all round one; and a new cemetery a hundred yards' distance from the house.

To this house and to this man the Ghost came.

And in this wise.

It was in August, when the days begin to close in early and it grows dark at eight. I was sitting, after dinner, trying to get sentimental over my approaching happiness, and picturing to myself Eleanor in the easy-chair opposite me. It was a feeble attempt at experiencing the pleasures of imagination, because I could not picture any one at all. Then I took a book and opened it with a yawn. My back was to the window, which overlooked the garden behind the house. The light was fading, but as my eyes followed the lines mechanically, and my thoughts were elsewhere, that mattered little. Outside the house there was a stillness extraordinary— no stirring of the leaves; no breath in the air; no voices from my own kitchen; no sounds from the houses on either side, which were locked up, their tenants being at the seaside; not even the distant bark of a dog, or the distant roll of a carriage, to show that there was another living person in the world beside myself. Then a curious feeling came over me: I suddenly realised the fact that life may go on in invisible, intangible forms: I looked round me with a shudder: I *expected* something. The room became, without warning, distinctly darker: the air grew chill: I felt cold dews upon my forehead. Remember that up to this moment there was no reason at all—none whatever for alarm. Yet I became unaccountably afraid. I turned to

the window for relief, and there—there I saw
IT, for the first time.

IT was standing outside the window, a
dark shadow, clearly outlined against the sky:
colourless, and yet its draperies were like
white graveclothes : shapeless, and yet, somehow, human in appearance. And it had a
face. Deep-sunken and lustrous eyes, bright
with phosphoric splendour, showed me hollow
cheeks, lips that trembled as if with passion,
and a frowning forehead. When I turned he
raised his hand and shook it at me beneath
its linen folds, and then, with that singular
movement remarked by all who had con-
versed and are familiar with ghosts—a movement in which the shape neither glides, nor
walks, but changes place—the spectre stood
within the room, facing me. I am not
ashamed to say that I was frightened.

"So," he said, with an angry glance, " I
have found you at last."

I made no reply. What was there to say ?

"I have found you at last, have I? Now I have you, what shall I do with you?"

I could only look hopelessly. He pushed one arm outside the cerements which covered it—a long, lean arm, marked with a tattoo representing a ship in full sail, surmounted by a skull and cross-bones. He shook his fist excitedly in my face. I noticed that the air was not stirred by his movements. It was odd, too, that I recovered my courage the moment he began to threaten.

His gestures became more threatening. He repeated twenty times running the question with which he first accosted me: "Now I have found you, what shall I do with you?" It seemed, indeed, as if he could say nothing more.

"Come," I cried at last, "this is fooling. What do you mean by coming to my house like a burglar and carrying on like a madman? Leave off asking what you will do with me. If you are a ghost out of his

senses, say so ; if not, vary the monotony
by saying something else. Can't you swear,
man ? Can't you relieve nature in the usual
manner ? "

He groaned and wrung his hands.

" I can't," he said. " It isn't allowed. I
wish I could. What shall I do with you ?
What shall I do with you ? "

" You have asked me that a hundred times
already. Bah ! you are a ghost. Ghosts can
do nothing. I used to believe that they did
not exist. Now I see that they do. But
look here."

I took the poker from the fireplace and
passed it through him. Then I cut him
down like a guardsman at Waterloo. Then I
sliced him in two like a soldier at an assault-
at-arms. At each pass of the weapon he
ducked, recoiled, and cried aloud.

" See, you cannot resist. I do what I like
with you. What can you do in return ? "

He raised his hand and struck at my

face. It was as if a cold wind blew upon my cheek.

"Is that all?" I asked. "Do that as often as you like."

"You are not afraid of me?" he asked; as if such a thing as a man daring to stand up to a ghost was unheard of. "You are positively not afraid of me?"

"I certainly am not."

"He is not afraid of me! Man! I am come from the churchyard. See my grave-clothes. I am one from the tombs."

I could not repress a shudder. The old shiver came across me. He saw it at once, and sprang at my throat. To my surprise, what was before as a breath of cold air became tangible. I *felt* his cold grasp with his long, bony fingers at my throat. His face, close to mine, was filled with an eager longing for revenge: his lurid eyes glared in mine: his teeth glimmered in the twilight. It was but for a moment that I was afraid. Then

I rallied my courage, sprang upright, and looked my spectral enemy in the face. As I looked the tangibility of his fingers weakened, the tightness of his grasp relaxed, and his look changed from one of triumph to that of baffled rage. Then he fell back sullenly, and threw himself into my easy-chair, glaring round the room.

" I never allow any one but myself," I said, "to occupy that chair. It is mine. Please take another."

He changed chairs immediately.

" Will this do ? "

It was one next to mine. I begged him to take one on the other side of the fireplace, which he did at once. Then I sat down, and surveyed the situation.

I was alone, save an old woman, my temporary factotum, in the kitchen. The people in the houses round were now all away for their holidays. I had a ghost, presumably a lunatic of a dangerous kind, under my roof.

It was impossible to get rid of him, unless he chose to go. You cannot push, kick, or throw a ghost out of a window or door; you cannot lock him in one room while you go to sleep in another; you cannot shut yourself up in your bedroom and defy him; above all, you never know what tricks he may be at. Thinking of these things, I became conscious of another *accès* of terror—slighter this time. My guest, however, perceived it, and in a twinkling was on me again, with his skeleton fingers round my throat. I shook him off; that is, I regained my presence of mind, and he cowered back to his seat, where he sat, his head on his arm, and his long white clothes clinging to his limbs, a sight never to be forgotten.

"Pray tell me what it means," I said.

"It means that if you were afraid of me, I would throttle you like a dog. It means that I am sitting here waiting for the moment when you will realise who and what I am;

the injuries you have done me, the wicked-
ness of your life, the loneliness of your
position, and your presence with another
world. Ha! ha! I see it coming! Your
nerves won't stand me another quarter of an
hour, and then I shall seize you by the wind-
pipe, and squeeze, squeeze, squeeze the life-
blood out of you!"

" You forget," I replied, "one thing. If I
find my nerves giving way—which is not at
all likely—I shall get quietly up and go into
into town. It is only half an hour by train.
They don't admit ghosts into clubs."

He made no reply to this. Presently he
went on again :

" You will have to go to bed soon. You
cannot sit up all night."

" How long can you stay here ? "

" As long as I please. Ho! ho! ho! I
can be with you, now I have found you,
morning, noon, and night. When you are
quietly in your bed, I shall be sitting by the

bedside, waiting for a moment's weakness. When you are at your office in the city, I shall be at your elbow, waiting to find you off your guard. At dinner I shall be behind you. You will not escape me. Sooner or later you will be afraid, and then I shall have you, although you are a bold man, as I know of old." (This was curious, because I did not remember to have seen him before, and he had one of those very remarkable faces which, once seen, are never forgotten.) "I thought I might catch you napping when I lit upon you here, all by yourself. Never mind! The time will come. I shall wait. I shall wait."

"Pray explain," I said blandly. "You will wait until I am afraid?"

"Precisely. We ghosts cannot hurt people who are not afraid of us. Our power is only over the cowardly and superstitious—that is, over nearly all mankind. Once the man has the pluck to stand up to us, we are powerless."

"Thank you," I replied. "After that I
will take a pipe. Can I offer you one?"

He shook his head.

"A glass of brandy and water?"

He frowned.

"Doubtless it will do you good to see me
take both. . . . Now, my friend, we will talk,
if you please. Do you not find it cold in that
light dress?"

"I have no other."

"Shall I light a fire for you?"

"No."

"Would you like a blanket or a railway-
rug?"

"No."

"Can I do anything for you?"

"No. . . Yes. . . Be afraid of me. Man!
think of it; I am a ghost! I am a spectre!
I am a spirit! I am a walker up and down
the face of the earth. When the dogs see
me they wail and cry. When men see me
they drop upon their knees. These are
coffin clothes! This arm is——

" My good friend," I replied, "let us enjoy each other's society without mutual confessions. I grant all that you have said. It is very curious and interesting. Not, perhaps, quite so horrible as I might have expected, had I known you were coming, but still—— By the way, you—you hail from the cemetery close by ? "

" I do. Ah, villain and traitor ! who put me there ? I do ; and as I was taking an evening invisible stroll, I happened to look in at your window, and saw the man I had expected and most hoped to see. Ha ! ha ! I shall make it hot for that man ! . . . So I will, too," he added, weakly, after a pause.

I made no reply, but went on smoking as if he had been an ordinary visitor. His face, which was not without a certain rugged beauty, was stern and lowering. He looked up occasionally with an expression of baffled rage which, now that I was accustomed to it, rather amused me. His features—those of a man under forty—were regular; his eyes were blue; his chin was strong and square; his mouth, which was weak, marred the general effect.

"When I was in that country ship, trading between Rangoon and Calcutta—there, what's the use of raking up the old story?"

"None," I replied, thinking that he certainly must be a lunatic ghost, and making a mental note of the fact as one likely to throw great light on the spirit world. "None at all, unless you like."

"To think that you—you, of all men in the world—never mind!"

"Certainly not," I said. "I am sorry you will take nothing. It is nearly my bed-time."

"When I saw you last, at Brighton, you were walking with her."

That was a little uncomfortable to hear, because I *had* been at Brighton a few months before, when Eleanor was staying there.

"No use talking. What's the good of talk? Come to that, I might remind you what went on, you know, at Yokohama. Eh? What do you say to that?"

"I have nothing to say to that."

"Lord! Lord! some men will brazen out anything! And what about the Hong Kong business? Who promised what—tell me that—if some one walked the plank, and something was thingumbobbed—eh?"

Here was a very serious question. I only shook my head.

"Thingumbobbed," he repeated. "Scuttled, you villain! and the coolies sent to kingdom come? And after that to round upon a man! Why did I take to drink? Why did I go off at thirty-six, with rum and water enough to float King Solomon's fleet? Why? why? why?"

"Can't say, I am sure. Shall we say good-night?"

"If you are going to bed, I will go with

you.   Man! now I've caught you, do you
think I shall leave you ?"

This was pleasant.

I shut the windows, and went upstairs.
He went with me.   I undressed and got into
bed.   Once there, I shut my eyes resolutely
and tried to go to sleep.   That was impossible.   Every ten minutes or so I felt obliged
to open them.   He was always standing by
the bedside, grave, stern, and resolute to do
me a mischief, if he could—*if I grew afraid*.

"You are still here?" I asked when the
clock struck two.

"Still here?—I shall be always here!"

I thought of my approaching marriage.
It was awkward.   A ghost for ever at my
bedside : a lunatic ghost thirsting for revenge;
angry at some imaginary wrong.   Could he
be coaxed?

I sat up and tried.

"Come, my friend," I said ; "let us make a
bargain."

" No bargain."

" You shall come whenever you please to my smoking-room, but not here.   Man alive! be reasonable."

" I am not a man alive," he replied.   " I wish I was.   And whose fault, I·ask you, is it ? "

" Come, my dear fellow, I put it to you— is it reasonable to intrude into my bedroom and keep me awake ?   Do you think it looks like good form to take advantage of your— of my inability to turn a spirit out of the room ? "

" Do *you* think," he rejoined angrily—" do *you* think it was good form to treat me as you did ?   Was it reasonable to send *me* to the cemetery twenty years before my time ? I shall stay here," he added, "so long as you stay here.   I shall be with you day and night. You shall never cease to feel me with you. I will make sleep impossible, and I will trouble your business hours."

"Then," I interrupted, "you are the most malicious ghost that ever walked.   I defy you.   You may go to the devil!"

He shook his head sadly, and continued that steady watch of his.   Always his chin upon one hand, while the white shroud flowed round him, and his face turned to mine with a remorseless gaze.

As I tossed in the bed, occasionally opening my eyes and seeing always that spectral figure before me, a strange horror grew up in my mind.   It was not terror.   I was persuaded that he would do me no harm, but the sense of being watched, followed, and haunted continually by this reproachful spectre fell upon me.   By some mysterious power he felt it.

"Ha! ha!" he said.   The laugh was not a cheerful one.   "Do you begin to realise it now?   Do you feel what it will be like?"

There was little sleep for me that night.

When the day broke I dropped for half an hour into a heavy unconsciousness, awaking suddenly and with a horror upon me that at first I did not understand. Between my eyes and the window, through which the morning sun was shining, stood a faint, almost an invisible shape. The sunlight streamed through it, and it was as shadowless as Schemyl.

" I am here," it whispered.

I rose and dressed. It followed my movements. I saw the spectre now only when it came into the sunlight. Then it was dimly visible, but only, I think, to myself. I breakfasted and went into the city. It came with me. It sat beside me in the train : it followed me through the streets : it was with me in my office : it came after me up the steps of my club.

The thing grew maddening. If I forgot it for a moment, I heard a whisper in my ear —" I am here." If I managed to fix my attention on the subject in hand, that accursed voice began to remind me that I was neither to sleep nor to work, nor to have any peace for the rest of my natural life.

"What you have done, I shall do—and worse. I shall dog you—I shall haunt you —I shall make remorse and despair do for you what you did to her and to me. I will revenge myself—and her."

What had I done to him? How was I to get rid of this accursed lunatic ghost? By what spell and charm could I lay him for ever in the Red Sea?

The full misery of the thing was yet to come.

The spectre, in the afternoon, seemed to have left me. I even forgot its existence, and dined comfortably. At eight I met my Eleanor, and persuaded her, not thinking of what might happen, to look at some new furniture in what was going to be our joint house. She came. Nothing happened until we went into the garden. As I led her up and down the walk, her hand in mine, she suddenly stopped with a cry.

"Alfred! who has been walking along the sand"—there was an edging of red sand to the gravel—"with bare feet?"

I looked. There were footprints—great gaunt footprints—parallel with my own. I knew at once what was going to happen, and I trembled.

"Nothing, Nelly; nobody. Who should walk in bare feet except a carpenter? Let us go in."

"Alfred!" she cried, "see, they are falling still—the foot prints—as we walk. Take me in—take me away!"

It was pleasant! The accursed ghost was setting his long feet beside mine, keeping step, so that at every footfall of mine there was a new footprint of his. I bore my girl half fainting into the house.

"What was it, Alfred? what was it? I am afraid. And see—see!—Oh! Alfred—Alfred!"

With a cry of fright, she fell fainting into
my arms.   Between us and the window stood
revealed that awful figure in its long white
graveclothes, pointing its long bony fingers at
me, but saying no word.

I took Eleanor home.   I implored her to
keep silence as to what she had seen.   I
soothed and pacified her.   I assured her that
it was fancy—that it was a trick of the imagination—that it was some schoolboy devilry—
anything to keep her quiet.   And thus I left
her, and returned, miserable and maddened,
to battle with this demon who had fastened
himself upon me.

He was sitting in my chair, with his
abominable head, as usual, on his hand.

" I allowed you to go away with the girl,"
he said, " because I do not wish to do her any
harm.   But she shall never marry you—remember that. ◆Wretch ! "—he rose from the
chair and approached me with threatening
gestures—" wretch ! Was is not enough to

interfere between me and *her?* You try to murder the happiness of another innocent girl! Can you ruthlessly——"

"Good heavens!" I cried, almost beside myself with rage. "What madman is this, who is allowed to revisit the earth in grave-clothes and torture an unoffending man? What have I done to you, devil or lunatic, that you should persecute me in this way?"

"He asks me what he has done! Think of Madagascar, villain of the deepest dye. Think of San Fran, pirate and crimp. Think of Liverpool Docks and Polly. Joe Morgan—Joe Morgan, you were always as brazen a liar as ever stepped, but I did *not* think you would brazen it out to me."

A thought struck me.

"You call me Joe Morgan. I am not Joe Morgan at all. I never heard of any Joe Morgan.

He laughed.

"If you are not Joe Morgan," he said, "I will eat my hat. I mean, of course——"

"Come, this is trifling. I say that you mistake me for some one else. What makes you think me Joe Morgan.

"Because you are."

"Nonsense. How long since you saw Joe Morgan?"

"Ten years."

"What was he like when you left him?"

"Much the same as you—sanctimonious look, reddish hair, stumpy figure, fat cheeks, just like yourself."

This was flattering.

"Only Joe Morgan did not wear a beard."

"Had this devil of a Joe Morgan any marks?"

"Tattoo marks like mine, on the right arm. I did him—I mean Joe. He did me."

I drew up my shirt and showed him my arms, white and free from any tattoo mark at all.

He was stupefied.

"Well—I'm—no—I'm dashed. And you ain't Joe Morgan at all? Lord! Lord! what a fool you must have taken me for."

"I did."

"And me to go and let out all the little secrets. Mate, you hold your tongue about that Yokohama business."

"I never thought much of ghosts," I said, "now I shall think still less of them."

"Go on," he said, "go on; let me have it."

"Why couldn't you ask before you came blundering into a house with your infernal long white sheet? Why couldn't you put the question before you began?"

"Why, indeed?" he echoed. "Look here, mate, I'm very sorry for this little mistake— I am, indeed. And frightening the young lady and all. I am the darndest drivelling idiot of a ghost. What shall I do now to make things square again?"

" Do ?   What can you do, but go right away ?"

"Shall I," he said, "shall I appear to the young lady to-night after she goes to bed ? I can easily do it, and then explain it all."

"Certainly not, on no account. You are not to disturb her at all."

"Well, then, I suppose I had better go."

" Indeed, that is the only thing you can do. Go at once, and have the goodness never to return."

He began to disappear. I seemed to breathe more freely. Then the shape, which had almost disappeared, started into sight again with a suddenness which brought back the horror which first seized me.

"One word, sir," he said. "I'm afraid I haven't come well out of this affair. Now s'pose—I only say s'pose—I can put you on to a good thing. It may be a wreck lying in four or five fathom Turk's Islands way ; it may be buried treasure ; it may be only a pot of money ; it may be coins, or it may be statues ; but if I *should* hear of it, and was to come and tell you, it might go some way to getting into your good opinion again."

" No," I replied. " I want nothing, except an assurance that I shall never see you again."

He sighed.

"Well, sir, I feel that I can't go against your wishes. I promise. No malice, eh ? When we meet again, which we may, there will be no malice, I hope."

Then he disappeared finally, and I have seen no more of him.

I have often wondered who Mr. Joseph Morgan is, where he lives, and what he has done, and how he managed to offend my ghost.

AN OLD, OLD STORY.

I HAVE always been of opinion that the treatment of ghosts by those other ghosts who yet walk about in flesh and blood, is unworthy of our boasted civilization. We regard with a terror perfectly ridiculous a race of beings whose behaviour has always been beyond reproach ; who have never had any crimes to compass, nor any selfish ends to serve ; whose appearances—singularly rare at all times—have ever been enforced on them by some strange necessity, or by the desire to accomplish certain definite ends.

The spectre who wrings her hands by your

bedside, dressed in her shroud—poor thing, because she has nothing else to put on—does not want to injure you.   Why should she ? And yet, at her first appearance, the miserable man who sees her sticks his head between his knees, stifles himself with the bed-clothes, and remains in that position till daylight dawns.   There are some ghosts who drag chains ; others who knock things about, ring bells, and make strange noises.   This simply shows bad breeding, but does not prove malice.   One is not *afraid* of a man who does not know what is due to social etiquette : why, then, of a spirit ?   Some ghosts are of a humorous turn.   These come round dark corners unexpectedly, and turn up when least looked for behind trees and in country lanes.   But we have wags in the flesh, and we are not afraid of them.   Whatever else they may do, there is no instance on record of a ghost deliberately appearing with a malignant or mischievous design.

They are a kindly, beneficent, well-conducted race, and full of good-will to men. It is in consequence of the singular ingratitude they have experienced for all their kindness, that they have retired, for very many years, into a kind of seclusion. Wounded and hurt by the suspicion, ill-will, and terror they have caused, they returned long since to their own haunts, and rarely put themselves in evidence. It will be found that, of late years, their appearances have been in almost all cases entirely accidental, and when they were taking the midnight air for a little exercise and change.

Very early in life I formed the project of vanquishing scruples which, I was convinced, stood in the way of much real—one can hardly say tangible—enjoyment. I aspired to the society of the supernatural. I longed to converse with the men *who have been.* With this object, I began to read whatever books I could find on the subject likely to

give me information.   I could find none.
Cornelius Agrippa and Albertus Magnus
may have been adepts, but they have left no
clue to their secrets ; while the ghost stories
usually told me, as I know now, were either
gross exaggerations or stupid inventions.   I
attended *séances*, only to discover that, if the
raps are made by spirits, they are illiterate
and vulgar spirits, evidently belonging to the
lowest social scale, and having nothing whatever to communicate.

I then tried haunted houses.   I heard of
several, and actually went down personally,
offering .my services to sleep in the haunted
chamber, and question the ghosts themselves.
On the only occasion when I was not treated
as an intending burglar, and permitted to
sleep in the house, I saw and heard nothing.

Accident helped me.

The way of it was this.   Six months ago,
my friend Philibert Jones deserted his old
friends, and created that vacuum which

nature abhors in our little whist-playing, pipe-smoking circle by marrying. I have nothing to say against his wife, who adds to the many charms with which Providence has endowed her, that special charm, which so rarely accompanies married beauty, of being civil to her husband's old friends. And one of the first things which Mrs. Jones did, after they were settled in their new house, was to ask me to run down and spend an evening with them.

They lived in an old-fashioned house, too large for a young married couple, but adapted for almost any number of interesting events, in the neighbourhood of Weybridge. It stood in its own old-fashioned garden, surrounded by a high red-brick wall, and was itself an ancient red-brick house, belonging probably to the reign of Queen Anne.

"I got it," said Jones, showing me over the place, "at a somewhat cheaper rate than such a house would ordinarily be let at, in

consequence of there being absurd stories
about it. The people round here have got
an idea that it is haunted."

" I'm sure we have seen nothing since we
came—have we, Philibert ? "

" Perhaps," said I, " it is haunted by the
ghosts of happy marriages."

Mrs. Jones smiled, and put her arm through
her husband's. I sometimes wish I was married myself; but the fit wears off. Besides,
I am too ugly.

After dinner—what a cozy thing a dinner
of three is, when everybody means to be
pleasant !—we took our claret into the garden,
and sat there through the long July evening,
while the soft twilight of summer lay upon
everything, and the sweet scent of the flowers
filled the air. And somehow we fell to
talking about ghosts. I found Mrs. Jones's
mind a mere blank upon this important subject; and I spoke, from the experience gained
by my own investigations, much to the same

effect as I have written before, in those valuable preliminary remarks which my readers
are already digesting.

The evening passed along. Eleven o'clock
struck.

"Come," said Jones, "this won't do—we
have been long enough over ghosts; let us
come back to flesh and blood—which, in my
own case, means a devilled bone. Lucy dear,
go in and get us a little supper."

We had our little supper—a devilled bone
—and then a glass of brandy and water and
a pipe, and then to bed.

It was about half-past twelve when Jones
took me to my room.

"You are our first guest," he told me. "I
hope you will be able to give a good account
of yourself in the morning."

He laughed, and wished me good-night.

Looking round the room I got into bed.
It was not a remarkable room in any way;
low—like all the rooms in the house—wains-

coted, and consequently rather dark. It was lighted by two windows, looking into the garden. I could not help thinking, as I got into bed, that here was a favourable opportunity for a ghost : an old house, which had been empty for a good many years; a newly married couple, who took it in spite of rumours about it; and a room in which no one had yet slept. Sighing over the small chance that any spirit would avail itself of the occasion, I fell asleep.

I do not know how long I had been sleeping—perhaps not more than half an hour or so. I was awakened by feeling a cold, gentle pressure of the right hand. I was lying on my side, you see, with my right hand sticking straight out of bed, as if to invite some such confidence. Directly I felt the pressure, I jumped to an immediate conclusion that it was caused by some supernatural agency. For a few moments, in the first flush of excitement, I did not venture, for fear of

disappointment, to open my eyes. Suppose
it should be only the house dog, or even the
cat. But no: no dog, no cat could grasp.
one's hand! I lay motionless. The pressure continued. I felt—oh, joy of joys!—
the distinct grasp of fingers — long, cold,
and, if I may use the word of what was
unseen, shadowy. I opened my eyes, and
gazed, for the first time in my life, upon a
Spectre.

It was of the fair sex—a young lady,
apparently, of twenty-five. Long light hair
—a wealth of it—floated in waves down her
back, and over her bare shoulders; her face
was clouded with an anxious look; her form
—not wholly, but partly transparent—was
draped in a white robe, not long enough to
hide her pretty feet, which were bare, as were
also her arms. The room had been perfectly
dark before her appearance; but you require
no artificial light to see the supernatural, and
a sort of dim and soft radiance seemed to fall

from her upon me and the bed on which I was lying, and the room itself.

I need not, I suppose, be ashamed to confess that, for a few moments, I felt upon me that irrational terror which men generally experience in the presence of visitors from the other world. My first impulse—which I resisted—was to snatch my hand away, and plunge my head beneath the bed-clothes. My next — also resisted — was to start up and stare at her. I may mention here that it is quite reasonable to experience this first feeling of terror, and that to be able to converse with spirits, not only without fear, but with positive pleasure, is a matter of long practice. Two ideas must be firmly seized in order to accomplish this mastery over one's self: first, that no spirit ever wants to do you any harm; secondly, that no spirit could do you any harm if it wanted to. At least, that is my experience. I lay thus, with half-open eyes, pretending to be still asleep, but

watching her.   She pressed my hand again
and again, but I made no response.   She
stamped her little foot with vexation at her
ill-success, and, snatching her hand away,
began to walk up and down the room.   I sat
up softly while her back was towards me,
and, at her next turn, our eyes met, and she
gave a little cry of delight.

"You are awake, then, at last," she said, in
a low, sweet voice.

Her voice was indeed the sweetest I ever
heard.

"I have been awake," I replied in a half-
whisper, "for some little time—ever since
you began squeezing my hand, which was so
pleasant a thing to feel, that I ventured to
trespass a little on your patience.   May I
ask who you are?"   .

"May I tell you?" she replied with
another question.

"Really," I said, getting bolder, "considering that you are here, that you have

spoiled my night's rest, and that you can hardly have come without some reason, your question sounds rather absurd, does it not ? "

" True," she returned, smiling. "What I meant was, that you are really not afraid of me ? "

" Not in the least now. I was when I first looked at you."

" How delightful ! You are the first Man I have met with not afraid to talk with me, since I—since——"

" I think I understand you. Shall we say, to prevent the trouble of explanation, since other days ? "

" Thank you—since other days. Even then men seemed to be afraid of me for my *beaux yeux*. Ridiculous, was it not ? " This with a flash of the *beaux yeux*.

" Not at all. I quite understand it. Was it—were the other days ong ago ? "

" You mean, I suppose, that I have grown old, and lost my beauty. Men were not so

outspoken formerly ; and it was not considered polite to tell a lady that it—— But
there—of course it doesn't matter what you
say."

She looked so seriously offended that I
hastened to apologize.

" Pardon me, I meant to imply that it
could not have been long ago, for the
contrary reason."

She laughed, and made me as pretty a
curtsy as the scantiness of her dress would
allow.

" I thank you very much. But it *was* a
long time ago—more than a hundred and
fifty years. You would not think so, I am
sure."

" Indeed, no. Is it possible ? A hundred
and fifty years ! Really ! "

It grew interesting. The little coquette sat
down in my easy chair, spreading out her
scanty white skirts, and leaning back with
an air of great enjoyment.

"I have not had a talk—with a Man, that is, for among ourselves it doesn't count, of course—all that time. I have made several attempts, but the stupid creatures always got frightened. Former tenants, you know. However, now you are come, you will be able to amuse me."

"Certainly, anything I can do. May I be allowed to—to make some slight additions to——"

"To your dress? No, please don't, or else I shall be made aware of the deficiencies of my own, which really cannot immediately be remedied. Pray stay where you are for the present."

But I was too excited to sit still; and, draping myself with the counterpane as gracefully as was possible under the circumstances—there is something, after all, of the Roman toga about a counterpane, properly thrown over the figure—I got out of bed. And then, turning to the looking-glass, in hopes of being able to catch a glimpse of my own appearance, I found, to my astonishment, that my visitor—if I may call her so—was not the only spiritual occupant of the apartment; for, sitting in a chair, dressed, like her friend, in a single flowing robe, was another young lady. For the moment my senses reeled; but I quickly recovered. What helped me more than anything else was a clear, ringing burst of laughter from the first apparition.

"Oh dear!" she cried, wiping her eyes, " I haven't laughed this hundred and fifty years. You *do* look so absurd. But you are a good fellow not to be frightened. Let me introduce you to Lady Bab Charteris, my very particular friend. Bab, my dear, this gentleman has the extraordinary merit of not being afraid of us."

As she spoke, the features of Lady Bab, which had been indistinct and clouded before, became clear and bright. She was a little younger and, if possible, even more lovely than my first friend. Her hair did not fall in ringlets and waves, but was piled and artistically dressed after the fashion of George the First's time, which I shall always love for her sake. She dropped me a low curtsy, smiled, and sat down again.

"Alicia dear, we are very fortunate. And now, sir, I must introduce you, in my turn, to her who had the courage to wake you up. This is no other than the celebrated toast, Lady Alicia Vernon."

I could not, stupidly enough, remember anything about a celebrated toast of that name; but that was my ignorance. I suppose my face expressed something of my hesitation; for Lady Alicia laughed, and said—

"I suppose you have never heard of me? Confess, now."

"I—I—am afraid——"

"Oh! impossible," said Lady Bab. "Of course, I should not expect to be remem-

bered so long"— this was said a little
anxiously. "Besides, a young woman who
dies at twenty-one, unmarried too, really
gets such a very short time to make a
reputation."

"We are both of us forgotten, Bab, my
dear," said Alicia, gaily—"of course, we are
forgotten. And if either of us were remembered, it would be you, my poor, unfortunate,
dear little Bab"—kissing her as she spoke.

It was rather embarrassing, all this. I was
standing on the floor, in the most ridiculous
manner possible—still with the toga of a
counterpane round me, and, as I was well
aware, my hair sticking out in all directions.
No man, not even the handsomest, can
afford to be seen by ladies with his hair in
that dishevelled state, like a Somauli Arab ·
at Aden, produced by the pillow. Why a
pillow does it, when a sofa cushion doesn't,
I cannot tell.

This, however, has nothing to do with my

history. I placed the easy chair for Lady Alicia, and invited her to sit down.

"Pray, do not stand yourself," said Lady Bab; "and if you feel yourself at all cold, get into bed. On the whole, Alicia, my dear," she added, looking at me thoughtfully, " I think he would look better in bed — we should not see so much of him, perhaps; and then we could tell him what we want, comfortably."

I made no objection, and once more retreated to the bed, where I propped myself up with pillows, and wondered what was coming next. It was all exceedingly novel and interesting, though the ladies would laugh whenever I tried to combine politeness with a counterpane. But no one, with a proper sense of what is due to the sex, can object to being laughed at by a pretty woman.

They both came and sat on the bed, one on each side of me.

Lady Alicia began to talk.

"What a real treat it is, Bab, to talk to a man again! Do you know, sir—what is your name? No, never mind your name—when I touched your hand, I thought you would probably turn out to be one of those wretched creatures that always shriek and run away when they see us? I am very glad you did not?"

"So am I," said Lady Bab, softly.

"All the good fortune is on my side," I said; and they both smiled prettily.

"I used to come here years ago, and when the memory of Lady Alicia was still alive, with a special object. Shall I tell him, Bab?"

"Why not?" said her friend, sadly. "We are both so clean forgotten now that it cannot matter."

"True. Listen, then, to a very short story. This room was my bridal chamber. It has been left exactly as it was—never touched or

repainted—on account of me and my ghost.
Over the mantelshelf was—for time has
effaced it—my portrait, painted by my husband himself, Sir Arthur Vernon.   He was a
good man, and I loved him ; but, like most
women, I had not married the man I loved
first, and perhaps best."   She stopped and
sighed.   " I knew, but my husband did not,
of the existence of a certain secret cupboard
in this very room.   It is here still.   This I
used as the depository of certain letters from
Charlie, which I did not wish my husband to
read, and could not bring myself to destroy.
I hid them away there.   Then I died suddenly, and the thought of these letters tor-
mented me.   I could not endure the idea
that my husband, or some one else, might
find them ; and for years I haunted this
chamber.   Lady Bab generally came with
me, in hopes of finding some one who could
be safely trusted with a secret, and who
would not be afraid of us."

" And you never found any one ? "

" Never, until we found you."

" Then," said I, " trust me. I am at least a gentleman. Let me be your confidant. Where is the cupboard ? "

She mounted a chair which stood in front of the fireplace ; then she pressed her finger in a certain place, and drew back the panel.

Behind it I saw two or three dark packets. " These," she said, " are the letters."

" Will you allow me to take them out to-morrow, and read them ? Will you trust me with your secret ? "

But she shook her head.

" Well," she said, smiling, " it does not much matter now. We are, as you have told us, so utterly forgotten, that a few old love letters make no difference. Besides, even if they were found, there is nothing in them to hurt my fair fame ; only they were not from my husband. But you may take them if you please, and read them first, if you promise to show them to no one, and to destroy them afterwards."

" Do you ever see him now ? " I asked.

" My husband ?   Oh ! you mean Charlie. No.   The fact is, that the poor fellow has been going downhill a great many years, and has become disreputable.   However, there you have my story ; and it is rather a frumpy old story, is it not ?   But, my dear, tell him yours."

" What have I to tell him ?   It is all told in a sentence.   A year of London, and routs, and dances, and cards ; a toast for a twelve-month ; and then, before even I had time to fall in love with any one, small-pox."

It did seem hard, and I said so.

" Yes," said Lady Alicia, " my case was bad, but poor Bab's was a great deal worse. And so, you see, we are a pair of ghosts ; and have been any time this hundred and fifty years."

"Yes," said Lady Bab, with a yawn; "and terribly dull it is, too, at times."

"But you have society?"

"Ye—yes. Oh, yes—there's society—of its kind: exclusive society: none but county families. The worst of it is, that one sees the same people always."

"Indeed! I should have thought there would have been a constant influx of new blood—I mean, of new spirit."

"No," said Lady Alicia; "not into certain circles. We retain our prejudices, and we do not like any modern importations. Consequently, we are rather hipped at times for want of amusement."

"*Rather*, dear?" asked Lady Bab.

"Very much hipped, then. You see, we tell each other our stories over and over again."

"But some of the stories must be very good."

"I dare say they are," said Lady Bab,

"when you first hear them. However, I never did care to hear them. When a young woman goes out of the world under such melancholy circumstances as I did, poor thing —and unmarried, too—she really has got enough misfortunes of her own to cry over, without shedding tears about other people. But you can amuse us, if you like."

"How can I amuse you? You have only to tell me a way, and I will do anything— everything I can."

"Tell us instantly," said Lady Alicia, "the news of London."

"With pleasure."

I reflected for a moment, and then began :—

"After the Irish Church was disestablished, and the new Reform Bill passed, Mr. Gladstone found it advisable, in the interests of the Liberal party—— "

"What on earth is the man talking about?" cried Lady Bab. "We want the news of the town. Tell us who is the reigning toast."

" Really, I don't know."

" Here's a state of things!" said Lady Alicia, with a sigh. " I thought everybody would know such a simple thing as that. Tell us the latest Court scandal."

I began to tell them all about the Tichborne case. Directly they found it had nothing to do with fashion, they put their fingers to their ears.

" It's very kind of you and all that," said Lady Bab, yawning, " not to be frightened at us ; but, really, if that is all you have to tell us, I think we might as well go away at once."

" Oh, nonsense," said her friend. " He must have something more. Just at present, of course, he is a little flurried by our unexpected visit. But suppose we come and see you again. Would you like to see us ? "

" Indeed I should above all things in the world."

" Then we will come here."

" No, not here.   Come to my chambers in
the Temple."

" In the Temple? Lady Alicia Vernon
in the Temple? Dear me, this is very
irregular! Well—if you don't mind, Bab,
dear."

" I think I should like it," replied the
beauty, "if he has anything amusing to
tell us."

" Then we will come.   Expect us—to-day
is Saturday—next Saturday, at eleven o'clock
in the evening.   You must be alone ; and,
if you please, dressed—in the fashion of a .
gentleman.   Keep the letters till then, and
we will be witnesses of their destruction.
And now, thank you very much for a pleasant
talk.   We shall be with you punctually."

" Stay one moment, dear," cried Lady Bab
—for her friend was already becoming indistinct.   "Do you"—this was to me—"faithfully
promise to be alone in your chambers ? "

" I do ! "

" No wild young barristers to destroy our reputation or compromise us, mind."

" I will be quite alone."

" Do you know what happen to those who break their word ? "

I trembled.   What could it be ?

Lady Alicia interposed.

" We need not tell him, Bab, dear— it would perhaps unhinge his mind.   But, my dear man, above all things, be faithful. Indeed, I advise it for your own sake.   We have no power to save you if your break your word."

" None," said Lady Bab.

" I will keep it," I promised.

" Farewell, then," said Lady Alicia.   She stooped over me as I kissed that slender hand which had no substance, and her long curls fell upon my head in a profusion of colour and softness.

And " Farewell " said Lady Bab, coldly

extending her hand, which I also kissed. " And, remember—*keep your promise.*"

They disappeared.

Lady Bab was, perhaps, the more regularly beautiful of the two ; but Lady Alicia, with her bright, smiling face and kindness of manner, won my heart, and has it still.

✳   ✳   ✳   ✳   ✳

" How did you sleep ? " asked Mrs. Jones, pouring out the tea in the morning.

" Never better," I replied—telling a tremendous fib.

" My husband tossed about all night, and had nightmares ; heard voices coming from your room—no doubt, in consequence of that little supper, which you might just as well have dispensed with."

✳   ✳   ✳   ✳   ✳

I had not slept one single wink. I lay awake with excited nerves and a chilly feeling, which I at first attributed to spiritual influences, until I found that it disappeared

on drawing up the blanket.   In the quiet
night there were no sounds at all.   In the
dark room there were no forms to be seen.
Could I have been dreaming ?

It was possible.   Meantime, I could not
sleep.   I recalled every syllable of the short,
too short, conversation, not one word of
which have I ever forgotten.   I called myself
a thousand fools for letting my visitors go
before the morning.   I remembered the
appointment for the following Saturday, and
I resolved to test the truth of my spectral
visitors by the simplest of all methods—a
search for the packet of letters.

I would not waste time by searching before
daylight.   I watched the light grow in the
east from grey to red.   I lay quietly till the
perfect day streamed through the windows,
and the July sun was pouring his early rays
across the waking world, and then, mad with
impatience, I sprang from the bed and began
my search.

I knew the exact spot where her finger lightly touched the panel, and I remembered how she drew it back with the greatest ease.

The exact spot I pressed. There was no result. Then I pressed harder still, but there was no movement of the panel.

Perhaps I should succeed if I were to get near the work. I moved the chest of drawers as quietly as I could to the spot, and, standing upon that, began my researches again. The panel was a piece of wainscoting, three feet long by two high, dark in colour, like the rest of the old room. The place where my lady's fingers had rested seemed to be exactly like the rest of the panel. There was no mark of secret spring, no knob, no button or handle. I began to think that I had been really deceived, and that my visitors were only part of a disordered dream.

Then I pressed with all my force, and I made a discovery. A small piece of the panel, an inch square, was cut out of the rest, and replaced with such dexterity, fitting so exactly into its place, that the lines of juncture could not be readily observed. It gave way beneath my thumb with a low grating sound as if of rusty metal, and as if the spring was out of order : it did not when I removed the pressure immediately return to its place.

This, then, was proof absolute.

My heart beat wildly. I expected the panel to slide back of its own accord, but it did not.

I pulled it, using the square aperture as a point of support. It moved an inch or two and then stuck. Whence then the apparent ease with which my lady had moved it ? I account for the noiseless and easy pushing back of the panel in the following way : There is a power common to spirits, and not possessed, or even understood, by mortal flesh. It is shown sometimes in the pheno-mena known as levitations, sometimes in the movement of heavy tables, sometimes in the banging about of chairs, sometimes in the opening and shutting of doors. Vulgar ghosts drag chains by the same curious power. It should be called Spiritual Force, and, perhaps, by a careful collection of the instances on record of its use, perhaps, too, by the voluntary narrative of such experiences as my own, we shall be able to tabulate and classify its results, to estimate the power expended, and to gauge the power possible. Like electricity, it cannot be understood. For that matter, what power can be understood ? And, like all natural force, its power is limited.

Lady Bab possessed force enough to move lightly with her spirit hand a panel which stuck fast; as it was, I could not for a long time move it with all my strength. I succeeded at length, and saw before me the packets I had seen in the night by the luminous glow which emanated from the forms of the ladies Bab and Alicia. I seized them; looked hastily in the cupboard for anything else which might be there, and proceeded to shut up the panel again as I had found it.

This was not easy, and when I had quite brought it back, there still remained the square inch of wood to which was affixed the hidden spring. This would not be persuaded to return to its place and I was obliged to leave it.

Afterwards, I heard, Mrs. Jones observed the place, and by the aid of the steps, rediscovered the secret cupboard. But this time there was nothing in it.

As for the packet, I opened it and began to read it at once.

Did you ever open a packet of letters, a hundred years old and more—letters from a young girl to her lover, and from a lover to his sweetheart? Nothing sadder than to think of the bright eyes closed for ever, the hopes gratified or disappointed, the tender thoughts which seem, read in the faded ink upon the yellow paper, wasted and thrown away. We forget their influence upon the lives of those who thought them first, and those who read them. We forget how maidenly trust and purity are strengthened, how manly honour is braced, by the belief that each has in the other.

Poor Lady Bab's letters were as sweet as any that I have ever read, albeit dressed up in quaint, old-fashioned garb, and talk of nymphs and swains. She thought she loved the man to whom she wrote. Very likely she did love him, though she afterwards married another, and learned to love her husband more. I should like to publish the story of that courtship of her's which came to nothing. But I cannot. I am under promise. I read the letters over and over till I knew them all by heart, and I have never forgotten them. If Lady Bab gave me permission I would reproduce them faithfully to-morrow, and then the world would be the richer by another pretty idyl, as sweet and fresh as any that have found an echo in the hearts of men.

I awaited the night of my strange trysting with singular impatience. There was a romance so unusual, so out of the common run of things in the whole business—apart from the natural desire one felt to converse again with creatures so lovely and *spirituelles* —that I could not even sit down till the time came.

The leaden-footed hours crept along. I had my rooms cleaned up for the occasion by a supplementary female, to the displeasure of my own laundress. I had got some flowers from Covent-garden ; and a small, bright fire—for, though it was July, it was a cold, rainy night—was burning in the grate. I could think of nothing else that would please my new acquaintance. Eating and drinking, of course, were out of the question.

Pictures and photographs might amuse them, and of them I had plenty.

The Temple was very quiet. Most of the men were away for their holidays, and my own staircase was entirely deserted, save by a hard-working lawyer on the first floor, immediately under me. In the silence I could hear him clear his throat from time to time, as he went through his papers. But there was no other sound to be heard.

I sat still, waiting. No one came. I put out the lights and sat in darkness, expecting with a trembling heart, to see the two ladies appear every moment. They came not. I waited till the clock struck twelve. I waited —with a dull, cold feeling of disappointment —while it struck one, two, and three; and finally, when the daylight began to shine in at the windows, I made a little heap of the papers, placed them in the grate, and with more sorrow than I can express, set fire to them.

One thing, however, I heard—a faint, trembling music—and a woman's voice singing. And these were the words :—

" Shadowy dreams and fitful fancies
　　O'er the sleeper's pillow flit ;
Not a night but has its glances
　　O'er the bridge where others sit.

Still believe that ever round you
　　Spirits float, who watch and wait ;
Nor forget the twain who found you
　　Sleeping nigh the Golden Gate."

No one will accuse me of ever having written a line of poetry. But was the song a dream altogether ? Or did Lady Alicia sing those touching lines as a farewell ? It may be so—for *I have never seen her since.*

LADY KITTY.

TʜE curious experiences which follow took
place in the most prosaic place in the world,
and the least likely for such a thing to happen.
Ghosts haunt old places and lonely places,
like chambers in Gray's Inn and the Temple,
where I have frequently seen them flitting
about at night. That is natural, and what
might be expected, so far as can be gathered
from the very limited knowledge we possess
as to the manners and customs of the spiritual
world. But no one would for a moment
expect the supernatural in the Liverpool
Road, Islington.

It is only by the young lady's own permission—she is actually reading what I am
writing at this moment—that I am enabled
to communicate to the public at large this
very interesting and valuable contribution to
our knowledge of the supernatural existence.

" Now, do not prose, but get on at once."

This is my Lady's own interruption.

I obey. I was a very poor man, and a
bachelor. Being a poor man, I was glad to
get a small house, exactly two years and
six months ago, in the Liverpool Road, where
rents do not run high. My house was a
semi-detached villa, as it called itself. It is
the smallest villa that ever had the impu-
dence to pretend to be anything but a cottage ; but as the rent was low, and my own
stock of furniture small, it did well enough
for me. The ground floor boasted of one
room, with a kitchen at the back. Upstairs
were two bed-rooms. I engaged an aged
female to come every morning at eight, and,

after performing the necessary sacrifices to
the Goddess of Cleanliness—very odd thing,
by the way, that there never was a Goddess
of Cleanliness in Lemprière!—to go away
as soon as she could. Personally, I prefer
young and comely attendants about me; but
the old and ugly come cheaper, and perhaps
are less likely to expose one to the breath of
calumny.

"Do *not* prose, I tell you," says the voice
at my shoulder, "but get on. We shall be
all night before you come to ME."

Well, I sent up my half a dozen chairs,
two tables, bed, and bath, and the rest of
it, and got away from my office—the place
where I was a slave to the tyrannical dictates
of a board of bank directors, without bowels,
appreciation, or generosity. A hundred and
twenty pounds a-year, if you please, for the
services of an imaginative mind like mine!—
for the discretionary use, between nine a.m.
and five p.m., of a pen which has written

verses for the "Family Teapot." A poor
fortnight in the autumn, with the holidays
of the Church, and the rest of the year
on the treadmill, grinding out the figures
which add up to such a tremendous profit
at the end of the year; and forbidden, by
a hollow mockery, to marry until my salary
should reach a hundred and fifty pounds
a-year !

> " Etouffé dans la foule,
> Faute d'être assez grand—"

Like many a greater poet before me, I bide
my time.

"If you do not get on with your story
and come to ME, I will worry you and keep
you awake all night. Selfish creature !
Always thinking about his own stupid misfortunes ! As if anybody cared to hear about
them !"

That is just what I complain of. No one
ever cared to hear about them. They would
not raise my salary ; they would not read my

verses—most beautiful things, some of them—
they would not appreciate me.

It was on the very first evening that I
went into my new house : one of those warm
evenings we had last year early in July.
I remember it was on Saturday, July 6th.
The thermometer had been standing at
84° all day ; and what with the heat, and
the hard work of putting up my bed, and
laying down the carpet ·in my sitting-room,
with the aid of the Aged One—who mostly
sat upon a chair and gasped—I was regularly
beat ; and after smoking a pipe at my open
window, thought that I would draw myself
a single pint out of the cask which stood,
newly tapped, in my kitchen. I drew down
the blind, lit the lamp, and took it with me
into the kitchen.

This was not yet set to rights ; that is, the
old woman, on being told to put everything
in order, had contented herself by piling the
few pots and pans I possessed upon the table,

and leaving them there. On the floor, by
the cask, lay some sand, which had been left
there by the workmen when they repaired the
hearth : of course, the dear old lady had not
considered it part of her business to sweep
it up. I looked carelessly at the sand, and
then, setting down my lamp, drew my beer.
On taking up the lamp again, I observed, to
my great surprise, the prints of two bare feet
—a child's feet apparently—toes and all, upon
the sand. They were side by side, as if the
proprietor were actually standing there at
the moment. It was very odd. I could
swear they were not there when I first
looked at the sand. Odder still, while I
looked, another footstep, a third, was printed
before my eyes, just where the sand left off.
Few men, I flatter myself, would have preserved their courage better than I did at that
moment of terror. I dropped the beer beside the lamp—putting that out as it fell—
and, with a wild shriek, rushed out into the

little garden at the back. The wall checked
my flying feet, otherwise I might have been
running to this very day. Brought up short
by the bricks, I turned to face the foe, if
there were any. Even a worm will turn,
and a hare stand at bay, if there is no way
open for flight. How much more, then, I, the
.poet, the man of highly strung feelings—
prohibited, too, from running further by a
six-foot wall. I stood with pale cheeks and
glaring eyes. Nobody! Nothing! There
was a seat—plank which did for. a seat—
at the end of the little garden. I call it a
garden, because the landlord did. It had
but few pretensions to the name, as it
boasted of neither grass, nor flowers, nor
trees, nor was it more than six yards long.
No living thing grew in it, save moss and
mildew. As these are undoubtedly vege-
table productions, I suppose the landlord
was justified in calling the place a garden.
I sat on the seat and wiped my face. Two

bare feet, toes and all—the feet of a child—
on the sand—one more presented before my
very eyes : what could this thing be ?

Robinson Crusoe's most fearful experience,
that of finding a single footprint—as if the
owner of the naked foot had been Jack the
Giant Killer or the hero of the Seven-league
Boots—was after all a mere flea-bite, so to
speak, to mine.   Anybody could see, I reflected with trembling, a single footstep :   I
would do it myself, with half an eye.   But to
see a pair before me, and then a third actually
formed before my face !   Robinson, in his
most lonely moments, never succeeded in
getting further than a single footprint.   What
could it mean ?

I suppose I sat on the bench, revolving
what to do, for half an hour.   Escape was
impossible, except through the house itself.
This way was at least open to me ; but what
a dreadful way !   I might, it was true, get
over the wall and escape through my neigh-

bour's house, and so, probably, incur the
charge of burglary. Even a ghost seemed
better than burglary. Then I began to
fortify myself with my own former experience.
Once, I reminded myself, I awoke, and saw
in the moonlight a female figure waving her
arms at me. After half an hour's suffocation
under the bed-clothes, I crept tremblingly out
of bed, and found that it was a feminine
garment—my aunt's—hung upon the wall.
Another time—but this was more fearful—I
was reading " The Spectre Smitten " in bed
on a summer's night. Suddenly the candle
went out, and simultaneously with the darkness there came a tapping at the window
—slow, measured, and regular : on that
occasion my sufferings were even worse
than on the first. I pulled myself together
a little after an hour or two, of the tapping
—which was continuous—and found that it
was caused by a huge buck beetle.

But neither of these experiences seemed

to meet the probabilities of the present case.

The situation was very dreadful. Alone in the house : no light, the lamp upset, the lucifer matches heaven knew where, the candles in the very room where the footprints were—and the memory of those bare little feet in the sand ! But the tooth had to be drawn. I must face the danger. Summoning all my pluck, I rose to my feet, and returned —-my nerves at the highest point of tension —to the kitchen. I found the candles and the matches, struck a light, picked up the lamp, poured out more beer and drank it, and then turned again to examine them. There were *five* of them ! I stayed not to look any longer, but hurried back with my candles and the beer to my sitting-room in the front, where I threw myself in an easy chair in an ecstasy of terror. Just then, too, my dog, which had been sleeping on the hearth-rug, awoke suddenly, and retreated to a corner,

where he crouched, whining and crying as
if in terror.

"Now, look here, you know"—it was a
girlish voice that spoke, but in cheerful tones
—"I am not going to have any dogs about
the place. I don't like dogs. So if you and
I are going to get along together, turn him
out first. If you don't, I shall pretty soon
know the reason why."

"Pray," I stammered, "may I ask who
you are, and where you are?"

"As for where I am, I am sitting on your
table." The dog was staring straight at the
table. "As for who I am, that's another
thing entirely; and I am not at all inclined
to tell you."

"Might I ask to be favoured with a
personal interview—I mean a sight of my
mysterious visitor?"

"You may certainly ask," she replied,
"and as certainly you will not get it."

"Are you a—a—particularly attached to

this residence, Miss — may I ask your name ?"

" If you mean, do I like living here, I can't say I do; but I'm obliged to live here; and my name is Kitty."

"Why are you obliged to live here ?"

" The first lesson I was taught when I went to school was not to ask questions. When I disobeyed, I got my ears boxed— like this."

Did you ever, swimming off the shore, have a jelly-fish strike your cheek ? You don't feel him, but you feel his sting. . That was exactly my sensation at the moment. I felt a distinct box on the ears, without any justifiable cause or reason for it, because nothing was to be seen. Curiously enough, the physical discomfort caused by the blow reassured my scattered nerves. A ghost possesses terrors which are generally per- fectly nameless. You do not know what he or she may inflict upon you. Given the worst, and you are at least spared the shuddering anxiety which attends the first spiritual manifestations. My ghost was young apparently, petulant, and somewhat quick-tempered. She could box ears. Would she also do anything else ?

" I must ask questions, you know. This is altogether such a strange and inexplicable circumstance."

" Not strange at all."

" Pardon me—it is strange to me."

" Then you are an owl. I am left here by my stepmother, and I am going to stay for three weeks more—locked up in this house with you."

" Won't you show yourself to me, then ? "

" If we are to talk, we might as well talk on an equal footing."

" Can't be on an equal footing. I've got no things."

" Never mind about your things. Appear as you are."

"You most improper person, I've got nothing at all on. My stepmother took everything to prevent my going out. So here I am. I don't care. Do something to amuse me. I am going to sit on this mantel-shelf and look at you."

I began to be provoked at her off-hand manner.

"I'm glad you've come. I have had rather a gloomy time lately—that is, for the last fortnight, since I've been locked up. Now you shall amuse me. Do something, I say—sing, dance!"

"Shall I read you my poetry?"

"Stuff and nonsense — poetry, indeed! They used to read me Dr. Johnson's poetry, and I always went to sleep. Sing."

I began to sing; but, as always happens when I exercise my light tenor, I was ordered to stop at the third bar.

"Dance, now—dance a minuet with me."

In vain I assured her I could not. She

made me clear away the table, and kept ordering me about for three-quarters of an hour. At the end of that time she was good enough to call me the stupidest creature she had ever set eyes on. I wheeled back the table and sat down. It was eleven o'clock.

" May I smoke a pipe ? " I asked.

" No, certainly not ; no one ever smokes before ladies. I don't like the smell. You may take snuff if you like."

" I don't like," I returned gloomily.

"Well, I am sorry for you, then. But nothing shall induce me ever to countenance smoking ; and as I am going to be here for three weeks, you had better go into the garden to smoke, or it's very little sleep you'll have, I can tell you. I like to make friends with people if I can," she continued ; "but I'm not going to be put upon or made uncomfortable, although I am prevented from showing myself by the harshness of a person

whom I will never forgive when I grow up—
never."

"You are growing, then?"

"Ridiculous creature! Do you really
suppose that I am intended to be always a
child? And don't interrupt. I say that,
although I am necessarily invisible, I can
make myself felt, as you know already.
How should you like to be pinched all
night?"

"I should hope, in the first place," I said
severely, "that you would not come into a
gentleman's room."

"Should you? Then you *would* be a fool.
A ghost may go anywhere, and through anything, without any breach of the *convenances*.
But I am sure you would not drive me to
extremities, and I do hope that we shall be
good friends while I stay. Now, your business is to amuse me. While you are away, I
shall amuse myself in the best way I can.
When you come home in the evening you

will read to me, talk to me, do anything but sing to me. At eleven o'clock you may go into the garden and smoke. It is eleven now. Have your abominable tobacco, and then creep quietly up the stairs to bed. Take off your boots when you come in, and don't make any noise, for I always go to sleep directly I lie down. Good night—shake hands."

She held out a hand, which I saw—a little white hand, cold, thin, delicate. It terminated at the wrist, and nothing else was visible. I held it for a moment, and tried to extend my fingers beyond the space where thin air began and the arm should have gone on. I received instantly a tremendous box on the ear, much sharper than the first.

"You dare to do that!" she cried. "Another such attempt, and we are enemies for ever!"

I humbly implored her pardon, and went into the garden. Outside I found my dog.

who peered curiously round me; but finding
I was alone, jumped up to lick my hand.
Nothing, however, could induce him to enter
the house.

Next morning, nothing: no sound, no
indication of anything being in the house
except myself and the old woman. Only
the dog kept in the garden. I went off to
the city with curiously mingled feelings of
pleasure, fear, and curiosity. I was, however,
resolved on one thing. I would keep everything to myself. None of my fellow-clerks
should know of my singular fortune.

The day's drudgery—nine o'clock to five,
let me tell you, with half an hour extorted
for dinner is a good day's allowance—over,
I got back, walking as fast as I possibly
could, to the Liverpool Road.

Not a sound in the house—not a sign to
indicate the presence of any one beside myself. I whistled to my dog. But, no—he
peered wistfully in at the door, and shrank

away. Next I made my tea and drank it, beginning to think that after all it was some strange and disordered dream.

Seven o'clock struck.

"Well," said the voice I knew, with a suddenness which nearly shook me off the chair—"well, are you rested enough? Have you had plenty of tea? You've been long enough, but I would not disturb you before. And now, put away the things and let us talk."

That meant, let her talk. She went on for four hours with a long and unceasing prattle. She told me things that she had seen; what her own life had been; and, though she was singularly reticent about her present condition, she gave me to understand that she was happy enough, and expected to be happier when she was no longer in a state of tutelage.

"I *came over*," she said—it was a curious phrase, as if she were an emigrant, but quite intelligible—" I came over about a hundred years ago, or it may be a little more. I was about ten years old then, so I am fifteen now, at the rate of five per cent., which is all we are allowed till we are twenty-one. After that it does not matter, of course."

" Oh, of course," I replied.

" And why of course ? Pray don't expose your ignorance. It's a great piece of condescension my talking to you at all, because my father was a duke—the Duke of Reculver —and I was Lady Kitty Reculver—you know *that* name at least, I suppose ? "

I bowed a mendacious assent, because I did not know it at all.

" My father was a minister. He was not a very wise one, I believe, from what I have heard since. But perhaps he was as good as most. I am inclined on the whole to think, though, that he was not so wise as the generality of people ; because, after my mother left us, he married my stepmother, the second great-great-dowager-duchess, you know. Any man who could do that *must* be weak in the intellects."

"Pardon me," I said, "but does it not become awkward, that kind of title—great-great-great, for instance. How when you get to the tenth or twelfth ?"

"Oh, we very seldom experience any difficulty. In the case of houses like the Montmorencies of France, they have adopted an algebraical method. Instead of saying great-great-great, for instance, they say great-cubed. This saves a great deal of trouble. Well, when I was ten, you see, the second great-great-dowager and I came over together —typhus fever, or something disagreeable ; it matters little now what we call it. I remember being a good deal annoyed at the time. So you see, by the rules, I am under her guardianship till I am grown up and can do what I like. When I do anything wrong, I get locked up in empty houses for so many weeks. That's my case now. A mere trifle, too—not fit to make a fuss about. What she called a breach of etiquette. Rubbish and nonsense! I haven't common patience with it. But don't ask me. We are absolutely forbidden to tell people on the other side about our life, and I should catch it tremendously if it were known that I have told you as much as I have. Tell me about yourself. Are you rich? No, I see you are not. Good family? I suppose not. Not that I care at all about it. There are not a dozen good families in England, and a generation or so is of very little importance to a Reculver. We date beyond the Deluge, you know, our ancestors having had the singular good fortune to escape by getting to the top of Snowdon. It isn't true, but that is what is always said in our genealogy."

" I suppose I am not what you may call of regularly good family," I replied—because on this point I am a little touchy—" but my

father was the rector of Muddleborough, in
Norfolk; and my uncle failed for forty
thousand pounds as a——"

"Parish pump and beadledom!" she
replied, rudely. "My dear good sir, do you
think I should consider you of a bit more
importance if your venerable papa—he reads
prayers for us sometimes in his new position
—had been a bishop? What fools men and
women are, to be sure! Go on with your
story, however. It promises to be as interesting as a novel. Oh, that you had one to
read to me now!"

I told her all my story, which wasn't much
after all; though, somehow, the subject
possesses the deepest possible interest to
myself. I had nearly finished, and was
dilating on the difficulties of living on a
hundred and twenty pounds a year, when
she broke in upon me, in her impatient
way—

"I really did not imagine that so extremely stupid a story could have been made so long. Why, man, don't you see that you don't get on because you haven't got any push ? What made the Reculver family ? The man who pushed his way to the top of Snowdon when the waters were rising ! I'm only a young thing of fifteen, with no more experience than a paltry hundred years or so can give ; but I know this, that the waters are always rising. And if you want to get out of the mire, you had better make a fight for it."

I shook my head. It was no use thinking of making a fight for it in the offices of any bank in London. All very well to talk.

" And haven't you had the spirit to fall in love yet ? "

Now, it was very odd that in the story I told her I had omitted all mention of my Emily. That was, perhaps, because I thought she wanted to hear about myself. Vanity !

Only the cases are very rare where ladies like to hear about other ladies.

I told her about Emily. Engaged for five years. Hopeless to think of marriage. Best and most patient of girls : also the prettiest.

" Prettiest ! " she said. " Rubbish and nonsense ! You men are all alike ! You think every girl an angel. Dowdy little thing, I'm sure ! Can she do anything ?— dance minuets, play the harpsichord, work embroidery ? "

" N-no—I'm afraid not. But she can make puddings."

" Ah ! very useful, no doubt, in your sphere of life. You don't mean—you can't dare to mean—that she is prettier than ME ? "

I ventured, with respect, to explain that I could not tell, because I had never seen her.

" Light the two candles, as well as the lamp, and you shall see."

I did so ; although two candles *and* the

lamp is an expensive job. I immediately became aware of a presence—a face and head, terminating where the dress should begin—with two little hands, but not the arms ; and below, on the footstool, two little, tiny bare feet—the prettiest feet that ever were seen. But ah ! such a face—such a beautiful face !—with its delicate little rose-bud of a mouth, its dimpled chin, its full, deep-brown eyes, and its wealth of long, dark-brown hair, that hung down behind in waving curls, disappearing where the dress would hide it ! A sweet child's face, or a face of budding womanhood. She looked at me, as Venus herself would have looked at Paris, with a smile of conscious superiority, of immeasurable superiority. I gasped. I fell upon my knees. I begged and prayed her to remain in my sight a little longer— only a little longer.

"Not so beautiful," I said—"by a thousand times, Emily is not so beautiful as you ! Oh,

Lady Kitty! tell me if all the ladies of your time were so lovely as yourself?"

"Not all; but some. The Miss Gunnings, for instance—pretty, but made-up, padded things! But, there, you wouldn't know if I were to tell you. So, my pretty lover, you are unfaithful already! Your Chloe is not so fair as Clarissa!"

"Nay," I replied, "not so fair; but yet I love her. We mate only with our own degree. I thank you always, madam, for showing me—what else I might never have known—what true beauty means. Would that I could see you as you are—I mean, as you might be—in a dress suitable to your rank and beauty! Oh, do not, do not fade!"

There never was a girl so kind and thoughtful. She remained in my sight for a full hour. I am not an artist, or I would have sketched her as she sat. But every line in her face—if her face could be said to have had lines—is deeply engraven on my heart. I can never forget her if I would, and I would not if I could.

. A whole hour! And it was not the only time that she condescended to appear. Night after night I was privileged to kiss her beautiful hand, and to gaze upon her lovely face ; till the features of my poor, good little Emily, down away in her Essex farmhouse, seemed coarse and rough to my imagination. Night after night, for three weeks—all too short!—she sat in my little room, turning solitude into Elysium and loneliness into happiness. The debt of gratitude I owe to her can never be repaid. But there was more yet ; for one night she said suddenly to me, without any kind of preamble—

" Roderick "—that is my absurd name : I was only a few weeks old when they gave it to me, and I remember I had not the courage to protest before so many strangers ; nor, indeed, at all, until it was much too late— " Roderick, I have had my term of imprisonment greatly lightened by your care and trouble. I have been thinking how I might be able to do something for you. The best thing would be, I suppose, for you to marry your Emily as soon as you can."

" I can't. I have only got a hundred and twenty pounds a-year."

" So you've kept on saying nearly every night, till I've really got almost tired of hearing about it. Well, you know, if I were older, or a scientific ghost, or a mining ghost, or an antiquarian ghost, or anything like that, I dare say I could give you a lift, in a practical sort of way, by telling you where pots of gold are buried. As I'm only a young girl, I don't know anything about pots of gold, and don't want to. But I tell you what I might do for you."

I listened with all my ears. Could it possibly be that my Lady Kitty was really going to do something for me ?

" We all take a particular delight in watching the fortunes of our own house. We do this, if I may so explain myself, by influencing the minds of our representatives. Sometimes we do this injudiciously, because we can't be any wiser than we are made, can we now?"

"Surely not," I said. "I know that from my own sad experience; and he who hopes——"

"But we may be foolisher," she returned, sharply; "so don't go on with what you were going to say. You are really a good fellow in your way; and if your wife only cures you of your propensity to prose and make goody goody remarks, you may turn out a useful sort of man, without ever having had very much go. Now listen to me?"

She was sitting opposite to me, in my easy chair: that is, her head was visible in the chair at the altitude at which a head might be usually found when a young lady is sitting there. I had got so used by this time to seeing the head by itself, that I thought nothing at all of it, and only occasionally noticed the curious gap beneath it, which revealed the chair behind. I should have said that no mistiness or cloud interposed to hide the chair, but that it was exactly as if nothing at all was there. Custom, you see, makes one accustomed to everything; and my imagination even filled in the flowing robes, for want of which the poor dear girl could not show herself before me. Her dear little fingers were interlaced in such a position as to lead me to suppose that she was resting her elbows on the arms of the chair. I may add that, after the first night, she made no scruple of letting me see her feet, as well as her face and hands.

"Listen to me, now. When any one of our house does anything very good or very bad, they say it is hereditary influence in the old blood breaking out. Very well; now I am going to show to you exactly what hereditary influence means. You only read the columns of the *Times* advertisement sheet for the next fortnight, and when you see an advertisement from the Duke of Reculver, take care to answer it at once. The young Duke has just left college. He is full of ideas about improving the estates and his people. He imagines himself to be an old feudal lord, with the interests of everybody depending on himself. Now, he cannot manage everything, and he will want a private secretary—that is, you ; a man of business habits—you ; accustomed to writing letters—you again ; ready to give up all his time to business—you, you see ; about thirty years of age—you, once more. Need I say more ? Yes, one thing more. You had better, in the meantime, study what I discover you are painfully ignorant about—the genealogy and history of the great Reculver house. And now, my dear friend—for we are in reality friends—we must part. My captivity is over, and I return to my own people. Forgive my little tempers and tantrums : I know I have them. When you go to the Duke's presence, I will try to be there and prompt you, if you want any prompting. Farewell."

She rose—that is, the head rose—and the hands parted. She held them out to me. I took them in mine, and kissed them—the prettiest hands that ever were seen. She smiled a farewell, and then, with the sweetest grace that ever gentle lady showed, she said to me—

"In my time, men saluted a lady on the lips. You may, if you would like to."

This condescension—so much greater than I had any reason to expect—overwhelmed me. I leaned forward, and with as much deference as I could put into my manner—it was not much, but as much as you could expect for a hundred and twen—I mean from a city clerk, and a good deal more than you could get from most of our fellows—I kissed her on the forehead and on the lips. Then I looked round the room, in a sort of bewilderment, and was roused by my dog's scratching at the door.   He came in, for the first time since my guest had been with me, and sat down as unconcernedly as if there had never been anybody there.

I bought the " Peerage "—a second-hand copy—cost me eight shillings and sixpence— and studied the famous history of the Reculver house.   Then I read the whole of the advertisements in the *Times* every day for a fortnight without success.   At the end of a fortnight—that is, on August the 10th—I saw the following advertisement :—

" A nobleman is desirous of finding a private secretary.   He must be of business habits, not more than thirty years of age, accustomed to correspondence, and ready to devote his whole time to his business, which

will be partly that of a steward.—Apply to
K., etc. etc. etc."

Now, anybody who doubts my story may
just look up the *Times* for that date himself.
If he does not find the advertisement precisely as I have quoted it, let him write me
down fibster, fiction writer, inventor, teller of
tarradiddles. *But it is there!* I answered
the advertisement instantly, setting forth my
own qualities, and referring to my directors
for references.

On Monday afternoon a reply came—

" The Duke of Reculver will be glad to
see Mr. Roderick Leigh on Tuesday morning, at eleven o'clock, at his private residence."

I got leave of my manager. I went to
the Duke's private residence—a magnificent
mansion behind St. James's Palace. In

trembling and trepidation, I was ushered into the room. The Duke looked at me— he was a young man of three and twenty— with curiosity for a moment, and then motioned me to a chair.

"You are acquainted with the House of Reculver, Mr. Leigh?"

"I believe, your Grace, I could even pass an examination in the genealogy of your family."

"That is very curious. You are fond of genealogical studies?"

I bowed.

"Well, now, a simple question."

When he first spoke, I saw the fair face of my own dear Lady Kitty smiling at me behind him; but this time I saw her whole form, wrapt in some wondrous silk that swept behind her, as she whispered in his ear—and he, as if speaking at her dictation, asked me—

"Can you tell me who was Lady Kitty Reculver?"

"She was your Grace's great-great-aunt. She died, about the year 1772, of typhus fever, at the same time as the Duke's second wife. Lady Kitty was only ten years old at the time of her lamented death, but already gave extraordinary promise of wit and vivacity; and was, besides, like most of the ladies of your Grace's family, of singular beauty."

"Very good," said the Duke, smiling; while Lady Kitty, behind him, nodded and smiled and clapped her hands.

He asked me a few more questions, and then dismissed me. As I bowed on departure the dear girl behind kissed her hand to me, nodded, laughed, and jumped for joy. As I was leaving the room, he called me back.

"Mr. Leigh, one moment. I am about to make inquiries of your directors about you. See this pile. It is a pile of 635 letters, all answers to my advertisement, from men in every position and of every age. They will all go into the waste-paper basket if my inquiries prove satisfactory."

I am now secretary and steward to the Duke. I know every scrap of his family history, and everything about his estates. I have been married two years. I am the father of a little girl. She is not like her mother at all, who has blue eyes, because her eyes are brown as well as her hair. I have called her, with his Grace's permission, Kitty. The Duke is the kindest and best man that ever lived. I am as happy as I can hope to be, but for one thing—I have never once seen my Lady Kitty again, though she sometimes condescends to pay me a flying visit, and speaks to me at odd times, when I am alone, and Emily out of hearing. I dare not tell the Duke, my employer, or Emily, my lord and—I mean, my obedient wife—a word of the matter. Oh, lovely Lady Kitty! It is not, I hope, infidelity to an excellent wife,.

to acknowledge that, while I regard her as some divinity too fair and good, as well as too ethereal, to be loved by a humble mortal like myself, her image dwells in my heart, and will never leave it.

THE OLD FOUR-POSTER.

On the east coast there are two or three fashionable watering-places and about fifty unfashionable. To one of these last, carefully selected as being one of the most unfashionable—only two lodging-houses and a country inn—I betook myself last August, with the intention of remaining there a month.

I was no more jaded than a man ought to be after a year of not too hard work, and no great amount of dissipation and society. My nerves were not out of order, nor was my brain giving way under that pressure which sets in with such violence about the end of the season, and of which we hear so much between the end of term and the beginning of October. And I was not contemplating an epic, or a novel, or a five-act play. I simply went down to enjoy myself in a solitary way —to sail, bathe, fish, stroll about, read novels, and smoke pipes.

It was about two o'clock in the afternoon when I got down there. The last eight miles of the journey were done in an omnibus, which they called a coach. One family was at my watering-place, and only one. I ascertained from my driver that I might choose between the other lodging-house and the inn. There were, it appeared further, no German bands and no barrel organs; there was no circulating library and no assembly rooms. In fact, civilization, with its march, that we hear so much about, had not come this way; though its tramp was distinctly audible not many miles away.

The inn was that pretty kind of inn which

they represent on the stage—a low, two storeyed house, with a porch, and creepers clinging all over the front. On the right was a little " parlour," as they called it, which was at my service; on the left was the bar, furnished with the usual display of pewter. There was a fragrant smell of thyme or of lavender in the bed-room; there was a garden behind the house, all dreamy with the hum of bees and the scents of old-fashioned flowers —stocks, wall-flowers, hollyhocks, London pride, and the like; and about a quarter of a mile away was the sea-shore, with a long murmur of waves.

The landlord, regretting the absence of his good woman, brought me a little dinner of some fish and a chicken at five. The ale was excellent; and after dinner I sat in the garden and smoked, in great content, watching the glitter of the light in the leaves till the sun went down, when I returned to my parlour and got some tea. In the twilight,

I went out for a stroll by the shore. It was very quiet. The family in the lodging-house were apparently all gone to bed. There was not even a coast-guard to be seen. I undressed and took a hasty dip, and then went back to the inn. Here I drank a single glass of brandy and water, and went to bed. You will observe that the day had not been exciting.

There were two beds in the room—which was much larger than one generally finds in a country inn, and extended along the whole front of the house. One of these, which I had not noticed in the afternoon, was a grim, dismantled, old Four-poster, occupying a good half of the room. My own was a little iron, bachelor's bed—one of the pretty little French things—but the other was a sort of ancestral state bed. That is, it had been. Now its cumbrous rigging was all pulled down; the curtains, rings, and hangings had been taken away and carried off;

the mattresses and valance removed; and only the four bare posts, with the sacking of the bed, remained. The posts seemed to preserve something of their ancient dignity; and it was not without pride—the last possession of a ruined gentleman—that the old skeleton towered in its fallen state.

I was glad to look at the contrast of the little French bed, gaudily painted in green and gold; neat and tidy; open and low—suggestive of quiet slumber and peaceful dreams, with a waking, early in the morning, to find the early sun streaming in at the window, and the twitter of birds inviting one to be up and away, plunging in the cool waves.

At present, however, the full moon was shining, clear and bright, into the room. I opened the window and looked out. I could see its long silver light upon the water, and hear the roll of the sea on the beach. There was no other sound—not even the

barking of a dog; and, with a murmur of
congratulation at having found a place so
quiet and so pleasant, I turned into bed,
and fell asleep.

The bark of a dog—a door slamming—the
sound of many voices—the tread of steps
on the stairs. What is it? I am a fool
to waken so suddenly, and a greater fool
for not going off to sleep again at once.
I address myself again steadily to slumber;
think only of soothing things; shut my eyes
hard; lie in the most comfortable posture.
But all of no use. My feet are wakeful and
restless: they kick of their own accord.
Something tickles my nose. Something
startles me just as I feel myself dropping off.
This evidently will not do. It has just
struck twelve, and there are yet three hours
before the dawn. I remember the advice of
Franklin. He recommends you to get up,
shake the pillows together, lay the sheets

straight, walk about the room for five minutes, and then try again. I get up, shake pillows, and smooth sheets, walk about a little, and open the window. The moon is throwing her light full upon the gloomy old Four-poster.

Broad daylight. A delicious cool breeze comes in at the open window, and awakens me. I sit up and look round, trying to remember things. Then, suddenly, I become aware of a most singular circumstance. I am lying on the bare sacking of the Four-poster.

A cold shudder ran through me as I vainly tried to remember how I got there. I could not remember anything beyond looking from the window, and noticing the moon on the old bed, and my own shadow on its sacking. A sort of terror came upon me, and I precipitately got up and retreated to my own

bed.   Then I gradually got warm, and
reasoned myself into the belief that I had
been sleep-walking, or had lain there for
coolness.   As for the troubled feeling, the
sense of something terrible which had
happened and been forgotten, I put it away
from me—it was the effect of a strange bed
and too many pipes.   I got up, bathed, and
came back refreshed and jolly.   It was the
loveliest day—a day on which a wanderer's
conscience would be soothed and quiet—a
day when London is hot and heavy, and
the Downs are cool and bright — a day for
a long walk to clear out the cobwebs of the
brain, to forget regrets for wasted oppor-
tunities, and to build anew gorgeous dreams
of things that might yet be.   I used the day
well.   I walked along the low, breezy cliff,
by the sea-shore, where I met no one but a
man who, I have reason to believe, was a
poacher ; at least, the ears of a hare were
sticking out of his pocket.   But he was not

a noxious animal, and answered me in a sufficiently civil, if not friendly, manner.

After some six or eight miles of walking, I came upon an old ruined abbey, with a small church of modern construction in its precincts, and a very old churchyard. Beyond the abbey stood a few houses of a village. The ruins were not much to look at. Three walls remained and the places where once were the windows; but of these the very tracing was gone. Ivy clung over all the walls and seemed to keep them up; but the abbey was long since roofless and desolate. I was reminded of my old Fourposter, and made out my fanciful resemblance; thinking how a mantle of ivy would improve the appearance of that venerable relic of antiquity.

Then I turned into the churchyard and tried to read the epitaphs, but I found nothing remarkable. In a corner of this God's-acre was a comparatively new monument. It was a tall and rather graceful cross of white marble. In the centre of the marble I read the inscriptions. They were to the memory of Charles Arthur Clynton, drowned accidentally, August 16th, 1838, aged twenty-eight; also of Lady Alice Clynton, his mother, died in December of the same year; and of Clara Helen Swinford, died about six years afterwards, aged twenty-five.

I sat down and thought of the mother's grief: died, too, four months after her son —probably broken-hearted.

And who was Clara Swinford? Perhaps his wife that was to be; and she, too, only survived him six years! Then I surprised myself with a big tear which fell copiously— if I may so express myself of a single tear —into my beard and lay there like a pearl. I am not generally given to cry over other people's misfortunes, being quite of the opinion that a gentleman can find plenty to cry about in considering his own. So, for fear of another, I rose and addressed my steps homeward, still thinking of the terrible tragedy commemorated by that marble cross.

In due course I got through the day. Making acquaintance with a seafaring man —not unconnected, as one may say, with the fishing interests—I accepted an invitation to go trawling, or dragging, or something else, with a boat and a net. I dined at five, had another stroll by moonlight, and went to bed at ten o'clock well tired. The first thing that caught my eye was the confounded skeleton of a bedstead, and I got into bed with words on my lips that should have been, but were not, a part of an evening prayer. And then I fell asleep without more ado.

What is it? I am awakened, not naturally,

but suddenly and rudely, as if I had been *shaken* into consciousness—thoroughly, however ; and I sit up in bed, startled, confused, and terrified. The church clock is striking twelve. The moon is shining full on the sacking of that preposterous great bed exactly as it did last night. And then the remembrance of last night comes upon me, and I begin to shiver and tremble. It is too absurd. I lie back, and try to get to sleep again ; but it is of no use. Curiously, too, the words on the tombstones are ringing in my ears : " Charles Arthur Clynton, aged twenty-eight ; Lady Alice, his mother ; and Clara Helen Swinford." Poor Clara ; Poor dear Cla—a— There's a yawn. I am positively getting sleepy again. " Also, to the memory of his mother, Lady Alice." Hang Lady Alice !

There are footsteps in the road : a noise as of men talking in whispers : footsteps in the garden, footsteps in the house. I cannot remain in bed. I leap out, open the window, and breathe the cold night air. There is a confused and shuffled tramp up the stairs; then along the passage. They stop at my door. The door, which I had bolted, swings open. What is it that makes my heart freeze, and my eyes glaze, and my limbs stiffen with a momentary horror? What is this nameless dread that comes over me? Why do I stand in this helpless way, staring at the open door? For I cannot move—I can only watch and wait. This kind of paralysed horror is momentary. It passes from me and I can again lift my eyes and turn them round the room.

It is all changed. The great bed is hung round with curtains, and tassels, and fringes. Clothes are hanging about. There is an old-fashioned toilet table, covered with brushes, jewellery, and rings. The chairs are littered with riding-whips, gloves, and spurs. The table is loaded with books. Lighted candles stand upon the dressing table, and the moon seems to have disappeared altogether. All this I saw at a glance, and then turned to the door.

In the passage were half a dozen men, adjusting a burden. Presently, they all came in, bearing—something! What was it? Five of them were rough, fisher-looking men, in sea-going dress. Before them came an old man, in some sort of livery, weeping. But they all had heavy, mournful faces; and all bore their burden in a reverent, careful way. They put it on the bed, and lifted the cloth. O God! it was a dead body!—the body of a young man—his eyes open and staring— his cheek pale and ghastly—his jaw sunken —his long, fair hair dripping with water, and matted over his forehead: a week ago, a tall, strong, handsome man. They put up his fallen jaw, and closed his eyes, and laid a handkerchief over his face. And then one of them spoke, in a hushed voice, as in the presence of Death's handiwork.

"I found him," he said, "off the Clewin Rocks. He was beatin' about in the waves, and his poor arm was nigh crushed to pieces. See here!"

He lifted the coverlet from the arm, and I saw—oh, the piteous sight!—the delicate, shapely hand bent over and crushed into the arm which, bruised and broken, lay upon the bed.

"I picked him up, but couldn't get him into the boat, till John Coss here, he come alongside, and helped me. D'rectly we got ashore, we sent up to the Hall."

I don't think I was afraid any more. The fear had passed away very quickly; and left curiosity, with a sense of something wild and strange. I waited to see what would happen next. Nor had I to wait long. Presently, there was the sound of horses' feet and carriage wheels, which stopped at the house. Then light footsteps on the stair. And once more the door flew open. Two ladies, dressed in black, came in. Their eyes were red and swollen ; but they had no tears, and no words of sorrow. They stepped quietly to the bedside, the rest silently parting to make room for them. Then the elderly lady spoke :—

"Take the cloth from his face. Let me see my boy."

The old man interposed.

"Don't ye, my lady—don't ye now !"

The poor old man. He dropped on his knees, with his face in his hands, and his whole frame shaking with sobs. I do not know which was the most pitiful sight, the grief-stricken old servant, or the wan-cheeked women.

But they took the cloth off; and the elder lady gazed long and sadly upon the features she was to see no more. The girl clung to her arm and, after a single look, hid her face.

At last she replaced the handkerchief.

One of the men, with a rough grace, took a pair of scissors from the table, and cut off two locks of his fair, silken hair, giving one to each.

" It hardly needs," said the mother.

But the girl hid hers in her bosom, with a convulsive sob.

" Come, Clara—come, my daughter," said the mother, and led her to the door.

As they disappeared in the dark passage, I heard the girl sob out, heart-broken—

" Oh, Charlie ! Charlie ! "

The bitter, hopeless sadness of the scene came upon me like a flood ; and, unable to restrain myself, I wept aloud.

Then it seemed to me as if the faces of the men turned to me curiously and inquiringly ; and then all of them slowly faded away and disappeared. I was standing in an empty room. The door was shut. The cold night air blew upon me from the open window, and my shadow lay, in the moonlight, on the sacking of the dismantled old bed.

Then I felt my heart grow cold and sink within me; and I remember nothing more.

Again I awoke, as the morning sun came in at the open window; and again I found myself, cold and shivering, lying on the bare sacking of the bed. This time I had no difficulty in remembering everything; and I got up, dressed, and took a bath and a walk to recover my nerves.

When I came back to breakfast, I found that the landlady had returned. She saluted me curiously, and inquired how I had slept. I thought she meant more than mere courtesy, and replied by a tremendous fib—

"Pretty well; but there was a good deal of disturbance in the night."

"There was, sir," she said, gravely. "And if I'd been at home before you went to bed —which I wasn't—not for fifty pounds should you have slept in that room—last night, of all nights in the year."

" And why not last night ? "

" Last night is the night when we hear the same noises, year after year. And they do say that it's the men. carrying poor Master Charles—him as was drowned six-and-thirty years ago—up to the bed-room where he slept the night before he was drowned."

" And have you heard the noises ? "

" I have, sir," she said gravely. " And I heard them last night."

" And did you ever—ever *see* anything ? "

" No," she said ; " I have never seen anything ; and I don't think there is anything to be seen. And *you* didn't see anything, sir ? "

I thought it would be very absurd for me to spread about a new ghost story, so I told another tarradiddle—a pious one this time—and said I had seen nothing.

Then she told me the story.

A pretty little idyl with a tragical ending.
A penniless ward, a fond mother, a handsome
son, a country-house. Put these simple ele-
ments into the kaleidoscope of Fortune and
shake them up. Shake them how you will,
but one thing always comes—love. Either
the boy loves the girl, or the girl loves the
boy, or both love each other. Either the
mother approves or she disapproves. The
end is marriage, or it is separation and un-
happiness. Our novelists are right in making
their tales turn all upon love, because there
is nothing else in life worth fighting for or
having.

This time the story was very simple. The
young man went soldiering for a few years,
as all young men of birth and fortune should.
He left at home his widowed mother and the
girl, her ward, who lived with her—a sweet
child of affectionate nature, who loved him
like an elder brother. From time to time he
got home on leave. The girl growing from

childhood into maidenhood the while. Then
his regiment went to India, he with it. The
ladies lived at home, and occupied themselves with their poor, with their books,
with such little society as the neighbourhood offered. Mostly they talked about their
loved one in India.

The day came when the regiment came
back again. Then Charles sold out and returned to his paternal acres, having had
enough of military life. He came home
handsomer than ever, and kinder to the
mother whose prayers had followed him for
so long.

He returned in June, when the summer
was beginning. It was only a week after he
came home that he made a discovery. You
may guess what it was. He found out for
the first time that Clara Swinford was not
his sister, and he informed her that they had
been having a great make-believe all these
years, because he was not her brother.

She replied that she knew it very well —but that she always loved him like a brother.

He asked her how, having no brothers, she could pretend to understand what sisterly affection meant.

She said she guessed.

Then he began to ask her what kind of affection she had for him. Did she think a good deal about him ?

She said yes.

It appeared here, on close examination of the narrator, that this duologue had · been overheard by the narrator's father, the old serving-man whose apparition I had seen. He was so delighted to find that Master Charles and Miss Clara were coming to an understanding that he listened for more.

Did she further think about herself in connection with him ? The question was difficult to answer, and required explanation. Did she, then, act, dress, and speak in some measure according to what she thought he would approve ?

Then she blushed, and said she certainly did.

Did she ever think about his getting married to some other person ?

She blushed again, and said she could not bear to think of it.

Then, her questioner went on, did she not see that sisters do not regard brothers in that way, and that she was nothing better than a little goose ?

She laughed at this and inquired why she was a little goose ? Master Charles, in answer to this, took her in both his arms and whispered in her ears for two minutes. Then he kissed her on both cheeks and on the lips; then she tried to get away from him, but he held her hands and would not let her go till she kissed him in return. And then, while she cried and blushed and laughed, he kissed both her hands and she ran away.

This was in the garden.

The sole witness of this interview held his peace, but he was not surprised to hear a day or two afterwards, from Lady Alice, that Master Charles and Miss Clara were engaged.

The marriage was to take place in August.

Why go on with the pitiful story?

He was fond of fishing and sailing. He came to this inn, the nearest place where he could keep a boat and find a man to take care of it. Sometimes he slept in the place for a night when he was going out in the early morning.

It was a week before the wedding that he came for the last time.

At four, when the day was breaking, he sailed out of the little port, he and his boat-man.

They brought him back as I saw.

His mother went home and sat looking into space with a shattered mind and a broken heart for a few months. Then she died. Her religion was gone. How could Heaven kill so good a son, so good a man? Her hope was utterly gone. Even her sympathy was gone—for she could not feel for the bereavement of Clara Swinford.

So she died, and Clara Swinford was left alone. She never put off her black silk; she never laughed, and never smiled. Her face which had been so rosy, so bright, so wreathed with smiles, so sunny with happiness, was set pale and grave. She was kind to every one, as she always had been; she was ready as ever to sympathize with every one's sorrow. But she lived alone. And, in solitude and sorrow, her life slowly wasted away. What a sad ending to a morning so bright and sunlit! In that dark street of tombs, where rest the young who should have lived to be old, where lie the early dead who by their death killed joy and brightness out of the lives of those who loved them, what more sorrowful tomb is there than the marble cross by the ruined abbey, beneath which lie the coffins of Charles and Clara?

MY OWN EXPERIENCE.

THE following experience occurred to me some years ago, when I was an undergraduate at Oxford. The college to which I belonged was of great antiquity and of the highest respectability. It had a creditable habit of turning out good men : it also enjoyed a considerable celebrity for good dinners, good whist, a geometrical bridge, a curious sun-dial, and an admirable collection of books.

There was one object in one of the upstair rooms of the library that, from my earliest acquaintance with it, had fascinated me. And so great was its influence over me, that whenever I was in that room alone I could not hunt about from one dusty worm-eaten oak bookshelf to another for the volume I was in search of, but I must always go and set myself opposite that object.

An old case, five feet nine inches high, not counting the pedestal it stood upon; rather clumsily made by some rough carpenter of elm wood, a wood supposed in country-side lore to have peculiar preservative properties. The sides and back of this case were very much worm-eaten; it might be two hundred years old—it might be three. The front was closed by a door hanging on stout brass hinges, with a glass panel its whole length. This door enclosed a skeleton.

The skeleton—to speak by the card—of one who had been a woman.

In earlier days the college had boasted some celebrity in medicine, and had sup-plied the University with more than one

Regius professor of physic. I had not the least doubt in my own mind, arguing from the known dates of our Regius professors teaching in the Schools, and the apparent date of the case and its unpleasant enclosure, that the bones were articulated at the cost either of the college or of one of these gentlemen for the purposes of illustrating anatomical lectures.

Tradition in the college, however, chose to assign a different origin to the deposit of the case in the library.

The generally received story ran that, nobody knew how many years before, a murder had been done within the walls of the college, which had stirred the Oxford of the day to the marrow.

It was a crime of the foulest and most unnatural kind it is possible to conceive: the murder of an undergraduate by a bedmaker.

Now, if the undergraduate had put his

bed-maker out of the way an excuse might
possibly have been proved for the act; but
this was killing the goose that laid the golden
eggs with a vengeance. Bed-makers as a
race have grown wiser since the time of
Mrs. Oyston, for the legend went so far as
to assign the name of Oyston to the per-
petrator of the deed. The name of the
undergraduate is not mentioned in this
history, neither was any adequate motive
suggested for the crime, but a particular set
of rooms was pointed out as having been
the scene of the tragedy, and it was added
that the deed was done as he was sleeping
in his chair one evening just as the supper
bell was ringing nine.

The story was told to every freshman
on his first appearance in that particular
apartment of the library. There were of
course many little variations in the narrative,
but substantially the bare facts of the story
were as I have stated them.

The library was opened for the purpose of taking out and returning books on two days in the week, and on these days our mediæval bed-maker's remains held quite a levee. Everybody who went into Dr. Smith's room, as the long gallery was called where the skeleton hung, opened the glass door of the case, and gave the wires from which the skull was suspended a playful shake. Impressionable young men made some allusion to the ghastly details of the tragedy, budding divines probably moralized on the uncertainty of life, the student of Shakespeare touched the worn skull, put his fingers to his nose, and said " Pah !" Medical students took the opportunity of displaying a little college learning.

Now, this sort of thing had been going in term time, two days a week, for between sixty and ninety generations of undergraduates, and must have been perfectly intolerable to the skeleton whose bones had fairly earned repose even if they had slaughtered a don.

I came to quite sympathize with the skeleton ; and in the librarian I found a man of the same way of thinking as myself.

I must describe him. He was nicknamed the " Tame Elephant." His build was extraordinarily short, stout, and square ; his muscular strength, as those who had seen him throw the hammer or put the weight knew, was enormous. But with this Atlas-like frame was found a very amiable and docile character. To this union of qualities he owed his *sobriquet.* His habits were unpleasant, for he did not love his tub, and was for ever changing his religion. He inclines to Buddhism now, I believe, after running the whole round of creeds. He was at the time of which I am writing a great walker, a great tippler of beer, and a very great smoker. If you were out for a walk, and a huge figure swung suddenly

round a corner, book in hand, and nearly
knocked you down; if you were startled
by somebody bursting through a hedge, or
fell over something lying reading in your
path, it was always the Tame Elephant.
If a light was burning at three in the morning in a room adjoining the library, it was
the Elephant still at his studies. And his
reading was of two sorts. He devoured
fiction in English, in German, in French:
his memory was prodigious, and he could
spout forth pages of Scott or Goethe or
Rabelais without a verbal mistake. But this
was his recreation. His work was poring
over the pages of every book on the Supernatural he could lay his large dirty hands
on. His knowledge of the University books
had obtained for him the post of librarian, to
which a scholarship of some sixty or seventy
pounds a year was attached.

A common purpose made us friends. He
had determined to penetrate the mystery of

the case in his charge.   For Wottenham averred that at dead of night, as he lay in his bedroom, he could distinctly hear footsteps in the library adjoining. ,

Whose footsteps ?

Presumably those of the ghost of the skeleton in case.

We determined to discover for ourselves. It was November, and a wild night; the wind blew—as it usually does in the introduction to ghostly narratives—in frightful gusts.   The *mise en scene* was perfectly appropriate.   We were alone, I and the Elephant, in his keeping-room.   He had drunk his usual after-dinner draughts of beer and had smoked several pipes from a huge meerschaum, the bowl of which was fashioned into a death's head, with superimposed crossbones.   We were in the oldest part of the oldest quadrangle of the college, where on the smoothly shaven grass plot ghosts might be expected to run about like rabbits under proper elementary conditions.

Our minds were duly prepared for manifestations by having previously—that is, between dinner and half-past eight o'clock—held an amateur *séance* in the Elephant's rooms, at which the manifestations had been remarkable. We are both firm believers in the supernatural. The key was in the door that communicated with the library to which we were about to turn our steps, and we were impatiently waiting for the supper bell to ring nine.

" Two minutes," said Wottenham, pulling out his watch, and puffing the last and sweetest cloud from his pipe.

" Only two," I replied.

Two minutes of silence. The steps of the old porter crossing the quadrangle to the bell tower in the screens.

Tweak, tweak, tweak. Then the bell rang out loud and long as it had ·rung out for several centuries at the same time, the only remnant now of a once, doubtless, substantial supper.

With the first sounds we rose and advanced to the librarian's door, as the oak planks that shut us out from Dr. Smith's room were called.

The key turned with difficulty, being seldom used.

Wottenham struggled with it, I followed and held a candle. His huge wrist and sinewy fingers soon turned the key in the wards; he put his foot against the door, and it opened with a bang. Rather, perhaps, with a dull, hollow, resonant boom; the sound the drop makes when it falls under a man's feet at Newgate. I, who am nervous and excitable, started at the unexpected noise.

Wottenham, whose nerves were iron, advanced with his usual rolling gait three or four paces into the dark room, through whose blindless, ivy-shaded windows only a faint glimmer from the quadrangle lamp penetrated on a dark night. Suddenly he turned

round, quickly for him, and rather irritably
snatched the candle from my hand. He
flung it from him, sending it literally spin-
ning into the room we had just left. The
candle fell on his bed, the stick into his water-
jug. I had time to reflect that the Elephant
was not a person of nice tastes, and to
wonder if, being athirst in the night, he
would take a swig, as usual, from his jug—
of water and tallow. 'Better without a
light!' he growled, *sotto voce*, in his stomach-
bass.

" You're not afraid ? "

Gold would not in my then state of mind
have tempted me a step further by myself.
But I had for company a modern Atlas, and
therefore managed to reply with some show
of spirit—

" All that man dare."

" All right; come on!" He turned round,
and I could see the white of his face, and
his not too clean shirt.

I supposed I lagged. We had half the length of the long gallery to walk; and our footfalls on the oaken planks sounded unearthly in the solitude and more than half darkness of Dr. Smith's library.

Wottenham, leaning towards me and groping, said—

"Give me your hand," and took my long thin fingers in his stout grasp.

There is great courage in a strong grip.

We advanced towards the case; and the only light from the quadrangle lamp fell full on it.

We were both looking at it, into it, through it, of course.

I seized his huge hand convulsively.

The wires were trembling, the bones shaking, the jaws grinning.

"We are shaking the old floor," said the librarian coolly. "The bones rattle!"

"No—not—through—us!" I said in a whisper.

The bell had just ceased ringing.

"Wait!" said Wottenham.

"Hark!" we both said together.

The steps, beginning by the master's lodge, came nearer and nearer, louder and louder.

They were close to us.

The bones in the case danced a mad and unearthly dance in their prison.

Our eyes, accustomed to the light, saw clearly. And the steps—the ghostly footsteps—walked round and round the case—round and round us!

Believer as I was, and prepared to find myself face to face with the supernatural, I trembled in every limb.

"Spirit," said Wottenham, "you are here!"

We paused for a reply. None came; but the footfalls ceased. A low whistling noise more awful took their place.

"We will wait."

"If you can ease your condition by speaking—speak."

Dead silence.

Then the footfalls again round and round the case.

The skeleton preparing a terrible dance—Macabre.

" Can you make yourself intelligible ? "

A knock which shook the dust from the elm wood.

" You can.   If we wait you will speak ? "

Another knock.

I had abandoned my grasp of Wottenham's hand.   I held him tightly round his huge body, and stared with all my eyes at the vibrating bones, and listened with all my ears for what should come.

" Is your name Oyston ? " asked Wotten-ham.

" Patience Clark," replied the Invisible.

" Is this your skeleton ?"

" It is."

" You are condemned to walk this room at night on account of the crime that is connected with your name of Oyston ? "

"Nothing of the kind."

"Did you commit a murder?"

"No."

"Then there is no truth in the report?"

"Not a word. In the flesh I was as peaceable a woman as ever lived, and the mother of eleven children, all alive when I left them."

"Why do you walk here?"

"For two hundred and forty years, good gentlemen, I have been waiting for the opportunity of speaking for myself and clearing my character. Now I shall not trouble the college, in which I hope I did my duty, again. I wish you good-night." The bones ceased to vibrate as she spoke. The steps, much softer this time, we heard running off in the direction of the Master's lodge. They went through the thick wall and have never been heard since. Wottenham and I did our duty. We did our best to clear Patience Clark's character, but we never told the story of her interview with us, for the simple reason that unbelief was rampant in Oxford in our time.

So much of my own experience, as yet my only experience, of being in actual communication with the world of spirits.

The Elephant — who is now a country parson—and I have been bosom friends ever since. But this is the only supernatural tale we have to tell.

END OF VOL. I.

LONDON   PRINTED BY WILLIAM CLOWES AND SONS, STAMFORD STREET AND CHARING CROSS.

www.ingramcontent.com/pod-product-compliance
Lightning Source LLC
Chambersburg PA
CBHW021037030726
47496CB00006B/1581